THE SOLDIER BOY'S DISCOVERY

Bonnets and Bugles Series · 4

THE SOLDIER BOY'S DISCOVERY

GILBERT MORRIS

MOODY PRESS

CHICAGO

YA
MOR

ISBN: 0-8024-0914-8

1 3 5 7 9 10 8 6 4 2

Printed in the United States of America

To Rex—
a real cool cat!

Contents

1

A Slight Case of Jealousy

Jeff left the thick woods and paused to look down on the house lying in the Kentucky valley below. Warm memories of days gone by flashed through his mind.

"I sure do hate to leave this and go back to the war!" he muttered. Then he shrugged his shoulders, hefted his flour sack full of slain rabbits, and made his way along the winding path, down the side of the mountain into the valley still misty in the early dawn.

The War Between the States had forced him and his family to leave Kentucky, which refused to leave the Union, and relocate in Confederate Virginia. This had been his first trip back since before the war began more than a year ago. It seemed sometimes that the fighting would go on forever. Often nightmares of Bull Run and other battles he had endured came back with sharp intensity, and Jeff would wake up in a cold sweat, thrashing around.

War hadn't seemed so terrible when, at fifteen, he had persuaded his father, now Captain Nelson Majors, to allow him to join the Confederate army as a drummer boy. Now, as he thought of how the war might last for years, he grew despondent.

His time with his friends the Carters was at an end. The bright August sunshine had brought a rich tan to his face, and he had enjoyed every day of his visit. Leah Carter and Ezra, the young, wounded ex-prisoner, were home safe; he could assure his father that little Esther was doing well with her foster family; and his father's troops needed the supplies he had collected. He couldn't stay any longer.

As he reached the foot of the mountain and made his way across a small creek that bent like an elbow, he cast a quick glance at the water, wondering if he had time to go fishing. He brightened. I'll get Leah. We can have one more fishing trip before I have to leave.

That thought cheered him, and he lifted his head and walked quickly to the Carters' small farmhouse. Going around to the back, he dropped his sack of game on the ground and pulled out his sharp knife to begin skinning the rabbits.

"Well, looks like you got enough to feed all of us."

Jeff looked up to see Mrs. Carter emerge from the house. She was strongly built, with pretty green eyes and blonde hair that was caught at the back of her head in a neat bun. She had been a second mother to Jeff Majors, and her daughter Leah had been his best friend since both learned to walk.

"Got five rabbits," he said proudly, holding up one of them. "Fat and thumping too. Nothing like a good mess of fried rabbit and poke salad, I always say."

Mary Carter looked amused. "I hope you'll let the rest of us have a bite or two, Jeff. You brought an appetite like a panther back from the war."

He knew she was as fond of him as if he were one of her own children.

"I'll go get breakfast started. I'm fixing you one of your special treats for supper tonight—apple pie!"

Jeff's teeth flashed in a broad smile. "Apple pie! Make one just for me, will you? I haven't had good apple pie since I first left Kentucky."

Jeff turned back to the job of skinning rabbits. Leah's mother watched him for a few minutes as she cooled off from the hot kitchen.

He was tall for his age—fifteen—with the blackest hair possible, as dark as a crow's. He had large hands and feet that he still hadn't grown into, and a pair of eyes so black that one had to look close to see the pupils. He had been stringy when he left Kentucky with his family a year ago, but now had begun to fill out.

When Jeff had the rabbits skinned, he brought them to the back porch, laid them in a row on the table, and then washed his hands thoroughly in the basin. After he threw the dirty water into the flower patch below the railing, he reached for the towel hanging from a nail by the back door. He stepped inside and smiled at Sarah Carter, working with her mother at the kitchen sink.

"Well, I've done my part," he announced. "Now, Sarah, we'll see if you can cook them." A sly look came over his face, and he grinned, "Tom told me to be sure and sample your cooking. Said he wouldn't marry a woman that couldn't cook."

Sarah, at eighteen, was one of the prettiest girls in the Pineville area. She had dark brown hair and very dark blue eyes, which she focused on Jeff now. "My cooking's good enough for him. I never saw him turn anything down of mine."

Her face flushed slightly.

Jeff knew she didn't like to be teased about his older brother. They had been very much in love before the war but now were separated for who knew how long; nothing was certain anymore. Tensions weren't helped by the fact that Tom was a sergeant in the Confederate army while Sarah's brother, Royal, was a Union soldier.

At once Jeff realized he was on dangerous ground. He said quickly, "Better get a letter written if you want me to take it to Tom. I guess I'll be leaving pretty early in the morning."

He walked into the living room where he found Mr. Carter playing with Esther, Jeff's baby sister.

Dan Carter looked up, and a grin split his craggy face. "This baby's a lot smarter than you ever were, Jeff. Why, when you were your sister's age, I don't think you had any sense at all!"

Jeff picked the child up. The baby stared at him with wide blue eyes, and he tossed her in the air, making her scream with joy. "I guess she is pretty smart, Mr. Carter," he said. "Maybe girls are just smarter than boys." He winked at Leah's father as he tossed Esther once more.

Dan Carter returned his wink and then, gathering his long, thin legs beneath him, rose slowly from the rocking chair, moving carefully as people do who have known much sickness. His once lustrous brown hair, Jeff saw, had faded to a dull, gray-streaked, muddy brown, although his light blue eyes still shone with determined pride. His mouth was firm under a scraggly mustache. He'd been wounded terribly in the Mexican War and would never regain his former strength and vitality.

"Not feeling too well today, Mr. Carter?"

"Oh, I don't complain, Jeff," he protested. "As long as a man's able to get up and walk and get some good vittles—and be with his family—he shouldn't complain."

"Guess that's right." Jeff carried Esther on his shoulders across the room to where an older Carter child, Morena, sat on the floor making shadow figures against the floorboards in the bright morning sunlight that streamed through the open door.

Morena's hair was fully as blonde and her eyes were as blue as baby Esther's. She smiled up at Jeff but didn't move.

Jeff reached out and smoothed down her hair, saying fondly, "I'll miss you when I go, Morena."

It always saddened him when he looked at this child. She was as old as she would ever be, mentally. Physically, she looked like any other nine-year-old girl, but she had never learned to speak and could perform only the simplest chores, such as feeding and dressing herself. She was happy, it seemed, and for a while Jeff sat on the floor talking to her and allowing the baby to pull his hair with her chubby fingers.

"I don't know what we would've done if you folks hadn't taken Esther, Mr. Carter," Jeff said abruptly.

"Why, it was little enough to do, Jeff."

"Take a tiny baby—for only the Lord knows how long? And with your daughter Morena to care for already?" Jeff shook his head stubbornly. "No, sir, it was a real big thing!"

"If things had been the other way around, your family would have done the same for us," Dan Carter insisted, sitting back down.

"No way we can ever know that."

"Yes, there is."

"Why, you can't go back and do things over!"

"No, Jeff, that's right." Dan ran his hand over his head, thinking for a moment. "But you can know how people are. I've known your folks for a long time. I'm telling you, you and your family would have done the same. Your mother—there never was a better woman!"

"I . . . I miss her every day."

"Only right you should, boy. And what would she have done if we couldn't have cared for Morena somehow?"

Jeff cocked his head to one side, then smiled. "She took in *everything*, Ma did—even sick birds and animals. Why, she took in a pesky baby fox once and nursed it back to health." He grinned at the memory. "The fool thing *bit* me! But she loved it."

"Yes, she was a loving woman. And what would she have done with a baby like Morena—or your Esther?"

"Loved her to death, I reckon."

"Well, there you are, Jeff." Dan smiled. "You don't have to keep on thanking us for taking care of your sister."

"It's a lot to take on, though."

"Not to Mrs. Carter, Sarah, and Leah! They dote on that little sister of yours—and so does Morena."

Jeff looked over to where Morena was looking down at the baby, cooing and stroking the fine blonde hair. He asked suddenly, "Mr. Carter, will Morena ever be any more growed up?"

"Only the good Lord knows that, Jeff."

"I wish she would get better. She's so pretty!"

14

Dan Carter's face showed a trace of sadness, but he said firmly, "We can't know God's ways, Jeff. But we can know that God is good and that somehow in the end Morena will be as bright and active as any other child."

"In heaven?"

"Yes, that's right. I kind of like to think of that time, don't you, Jeff?"

"You mean . . . heaven? When we get there?"

"Yes." Dan smiled and added, "No wars, no droughts, no need for doctors—no politicians, either. Not like this place."

Jeff's face clouded as he thought through Mr. Carter's comments. Finally he replied, "I guess I'm not a good enough Christian."

"Why do you say that?"

"Well, I guess I'm not ready to go to heaven—not today, I mean."

Mr. Carter laughed, and his eyes twinkled. "Enjoy the day, for the Lord has given it to us. 'This is the day that the Lord hath made. We will rejoice and be glad in it.' We can't know when we'll go, so we live for the Lord here until we go there."

Jeff didn't reply, his face darkening as thoughts of heaven led to thoughts of death—and how the war had brought death close to so many over the last year. He finally said, "Well, Ezra's out of the war, anyway. He won't have to fight anymore. Nobody wants a convalescing ex-prisoner of war on his front lines."

"Yes, and I'm glad of it. I wish you were out too."

"Me too, and Pa and Tom—and Royal, of course."

"You know, Jeff, I think God put Ezra in that prison camp."

"What for?" Jeff asked with surprise.

"Well, look at it," Dan said slowly. "I can't go off with Leah and leave this farm all the time with Mrs. Carter and Sarah and the children all alone, can I?"

"No, sir, I don't think you can."

"Well, it's hard to find good help for a small farm. I tried pretty hard, and all I could come up with was hiring Ray Studdard from across the way. I couldn't see doing anything else, as expensive as that would be. But here Ezra escapes from that Confederate prison camp, and he hides out in a farmhouse. How many farmhouses are there in that part of the country, Jeff?"

"Must be a thousand, Mr. Carter."

"Yep, I'd say so. Ezra could have gone to any one of them. But he didn't. He went to the *only* one where he'd have a chance to meet Leah. Now, that just *couldn't* have been an accident!"

Jeff stared. "You think God does stuff like that? I mean . . . that He works things out for us?"

"He knows of the sparrow's fall, Jeff, and we're worth more than sparrows."

Jeff shifted restlessly, then shook his head. "Too much for me to figure out," he said finally. "Do you reckon Ezra will stay on for a long time?"

"The boy's got no place else to go." Mr. Carter shrugged. "Why are you asking, Jeff?"

"Oh, no reason. Just wondering."

Jeff's thoughts moved from Ezra—and Ezra's budding friendship with Leah—to what a fine man Dan Carter was.

Even though he was too old for the army, and too sickly, he'd determined to do his best for the soldiers in the Union army. He'd persuaded his family that he should serve God by becoming a sutler, stocking his old wagon with supplies—including Bibles and tracts—and following the Yankee army throughout the first year of the war. He'd taken Leah with him because, even though she was just a young girl, she was strong, healthy, and smart. Especially when he had his bad spells, she took much of the work off his shoulders.

Jeff looked about as he started to get up from the floor by Morena and Esther. "Where's Leah?"

"Oh, she's gone with Ezra. I think they went hunting birds' eggs, Jeff." He stopped abruptly, looking at Jeff's face.

The boy scooped up Esther. He swung her under his arm as he strode across the room and dumped her into Dan's arms. He muttered, "Should of known she'd rather hunt eggs than fish with me." He left the room without another word.

Almost as soon as Jeff had passed through the door, Mrs. Carter entered, her hands white with flour. Looking around, she asked with surprise, "Where's Jeff off to?"

"He just lit out after Leah and Ezra," Dan said. He gave his wife a look and shook his head. "I think he's a little bit upset."

"Upset about what?"

"Oh, I told him Ezra and Leah had gone egg hunting, and he clammed up and left with hardly a word."

She went over and looked out the window. She saw Jeff stalking off, his back straight and his steps almost military. Shaking her head, she turned back and said quietly, "Jeff hasn't taken much to Ezra. You'd think they would've become friends after Jeff helped Leah hide him the way he did."

Ezra Payne had served in the Union army and was taken captive at the Battle of Bull Run. He had escaped from prison, and Leah and Jeff helped him get away to Kentucky.

"Well, you know how strong Jeff is about Confederate rights, Mary. Might be he can't get over Ezra being a Union soldier." Mr. Carter paused. "It's not like our Royal—or even my sutler work. Jeff's been like part of our family his whole life, but he don't have any history with Ezra."

"You're at least right on that account, Dan," she agreed. "Remember Leah told us about the set-to she and Jeff had when she first asked him to help her with Ezra."

"I don't know what's going to come of this." He shook his head. "Jeff's a good boy, but he's got hard feelings against the North."

"That's not the main cause of it, though," his wife murmured. She dusted the flour off her hands as she crossed the room, and then she lifted Esther out of Dan's lap. She pinched the baby's fat, rosy cheek, then turned to give her husband a direct look. "He's jealous of Ezra. I guess you see that, Dan. They've been awfully close, Leah and Jeff, all their lives."

"Why, they're only children!"

"I guess you don't have to be fifty years old to get possessive of somebody. Leah would be just as possessive of Jeff. I'm sorry for it, though Ezra is a fine young man. He hasn't had much of a chance in this world."

18

"No, he hasn't." Mr. Carter shook his head as he remembered what Ezra had told them. "Nobody should have to spend his childhood an orphan, working like a slave on some stranger's farm."

"I'm grateful we can give him some of the love he's never had." Mrs. Carter's voice came with conviction.

"But Mary, neither one of us wants Jeff hurt over Leah," he protested. "Maybe we ought not to ask Ezra to stay."

"Oh, we've got to! We promised. We can't abandon him. Besides, you said yourself God brought him to give us the help we need now that Royal's off to the war. Ezra's such a good worker." She put the baby down and sighed heavily. "Well, I have every confidence our prayers and Jeff's basic good sense will make the difference. Jeff's a good boy—he'll just have to get over this."

"Look! What's this one, Leah?"

Leah Carter looked up into the thick foliage of the oak tree. She squinted at the egg Ezra was holding and said, "I can't tell. Bring it on down."

"Do you want all of them?"

"No, just one. Leave the rest to hatch."

Ezra Payne came down the tree, swinging from branch to branch, using only one hand.

When he jumped to the ground, Leah laughed at him. "You're just like a monkey, Ezra! I've never seen anyone who could climb a tree like you."

Ezra smiled at the girl. He was not tall, but when he regained the weight he'd lost, he would present a formidable set of muscles to any opponent. His curly brown hair and sparkling teeth were in sharp contrast to his pale prison complexion.

"Always liked to climb trees!" he said. "When I was with the army, they'd send me to the top of the tallest tree so's I could scout out the enemy. Why, one time General McClellan himself was down at the foot with his officers." He grinned more broadly, "There I was, telling the general of the whole Union army how it was!"

Leah laughed again as she took the egg. "That's just another story you're making up. Let me see that egg." She ignored his protests of innocence, studied the egg, and announced, "That's a catbird egg. We've got plenty of those."

"Have I got to take it back up to the nest?"

"Of course. You're not going to eat it raw!"

"I've seen the day I would, like when you found me stealing your groceries back in Virginia."

"That's different." Leah shrugged. She smiled at him suddenly, adding, "You weren't a very good burglar, Ezra. You made more noise than a wild pig."

"Didn't have much experience."

"I hope you never get any more."

Ezra climbed the tree and replaced the egg. When he was back on the ground, he affectionately slapped Leah on the shoulder and declared, "You must know every bird's egg there is, Leah."

"I ought to—been hunting them most of my life. Come on, let's go down by the river. Maybe we'll find a kingfisher nest. They're sure hard to find."

The two of them picked their way down a path overgrown with summer ferns, vines, and saplings until they came to the creek. Leah chattered happily all the time, telling Ezra about birds of all kinds. Finally she turned to him and exclaimed, "I'm so glad you've come to stay with our family, Ezra. With my brother, Royal, gone to the army, the farm's about to fall to pieces. My folks say you're an answer to prayer. "

Ezra glanced at her quickly. His face grew serious. "Well, it's about the best thing that's ever happened to me, Leah. You can't know how different it is to work because you belong instead of just to get out of a beating."

He looked at the trees surrounding them and cocked his head, seeming to listen to the creek bubbling at their feet, before he said, "I've never had a home, not a real one anyhow—just living with people, and then the army—and then prison camp."

"My folks think a lot of you."

"I never met anyone kinder."

"They're special, all right."

"You're sure lucky, Leah, to have good parents like them."

Leah glanced quickly into his face and saw the honesty there. Honest pain and honest yearning. She was glad she'd helped Ezra escape from Virginia. He had been so sick that she thought he wouldn't live. Now she said quickly, "Well, it's good for everybody."

Ezra fell in beside her as they walked along the creek, saying nothing for a while. Finally Ezra said, "I'm afraid Jeff doesn't like it too much."

Leah shot a glance at him. "He'll be all right. Jeff just doesn't warm up to people right away sometimes."

"I like him fine, but he just doesn't take to me."

"Jeff's too fast to make up his mind, I think. He does everything quick. He gets mad sometimes, then he's over it in a flash and feels bad about it. Don't worry about it, Ezra."

They followed the creek for a while as it cut through the valley, then took a game trail across the meadow back toward the lane leading to the farmhouse. As they rounded the last bend, Ezra peered ahead, exclaiming, "Look! There's Jeff now."

Leah watched Jeff stride toward them down the lane. She could tell at a glance that he was angry. His long legs ate up the distance, and his fists were balled at his sides.

Leah's voice betrayed her worry. "We've been gone longer than I thought, but he shouldn't be mad. He's the one who wanted to go hunting by himself while it was still dark." Jeff pointedly ignored Ezra and focused on Leah's face. "I've been looking for you."

"I'm glad you got back, Jeff. Did you get any rabbits?"

"A few," he said shortly. "I thought we were going fishing?"

"Oh, Jeff, I didn't think you would be back in time."

"I was back in plenty of time."

"Well, it's still not too late." She rested her hand on his arm. "Let's go later this afternoon when the sun's not so hot. We can catch a few before supper." Still grasping Jeff's arm, she turned to Ezra. "You can come too, Ezra."

"No, it's too late now." Jeff pulled his arm away, turned without another word, and loped down the road.

Leah whispered urgently, "Ezra, he's upset. Let me go talk to him." She ran quickly and caught up with Jeff, half skipping to keep up with his long strides. "Don't walk so fast," she pleaded, pulling on his arm to slow his pace.

Jeff paused, his face flushed. His lips were drawn tightly together, and he wouldn't look at her.

Leah bit her lip. She was annoyed. After all, he had been the one to leave and go hunting alone. Now she said sharply, "Jeff, don't be like that. We still have time to go fishing—and we can go run a trotline down by the rocks tonight."

"No, I guess not."

"You're just being stubborn." She pulled him to a stop, and he turned to face her.

What Jeff saw was a young woman of fourteen with green eyes and blonde hair. She was tall for a girl and had sometimes complained that she was as tall as a crane. Jeff noticed that she had filled out a great deal since he had left and had become far more like a young woman than the scrawny girl he had left behind.

He said shortly, "I don't know why you have to spend all your time with him!"

"Jeff, you're just being silly."

"I don't think it's silly. He's the enemy, Leah. He's fighting for the North."

"Well, so is Royal, if you'll remember. We've been over all this before. Besides, Ezra's not fighting for anybody now."

Hot words began to fall from their lips. Both had tempers, and, while they were growing up, more than one fiery argument had separated them for a time. They usually got over it pretty quickly, but this time Jeff refused to be pacified. Finally, he made a big mistake. He blurted out, "You're nothing but a Yankee, Leah Carter!"

This raised Leah's temper another notch, and she shot back, tears in her eyes, "Well, if I'm a Yankee, then you're nothing but a ragtag Rebel!" She turned and ran down the road toward the house.

He stood watching her go, feeling about as miserable as he ever had in his life, but he was too stubborn to admit it. "Well, if that's the way she wants to be, she can just have Ezra Payne and the whole Union army!"

2
"We Must Obey God!"

Jeff took his seat at the breakfast table, his face red and flushed from the vigorous washing he'd given it on the back porch. He didn't glance at Leah but bowed his head while Mr. Carter asked the blessing. As soon as the Amen was said, he allowed Mrs. Carter to fill his plate with eggs, ham, and fried potatoes. He began to eat at once, stubbornly keeping his eyes down.

Dan Carter didn't miss this and glanced at Leah, whose face was rather pale. Then he glanced at Ezra, who was eating more slowly than usual. "I sure am glad you've come to help," he said cheerfully. "This place was going down quick. It needs a strong young man like you to keep it up."

Ezra glanced up. "Why, I haven't gotten started yet, Mr. Carter. You just wait—I'll make this farm hum!"

Mary Carter smiled at the young man. "You're a good hand, Ezra. Never saw anyone work harder."

"Well, I like to work on a farm." Ezra smiled shyly. "Never was on such a nice place as this one."

"I think you know every foot of it, Ezra," Sarah said. She had said she liked Ezra from the start, and now added, "It makes a big difference having a man on the place."

Leah glanced at Jeff and saw that he was looking down at his plate. They had ignored each other since their argument, and she was finally willing to take the first step toward making up. "Jeff knows the farm as well as anybody," she offered, but Jeff didn't lift his eyes.

Her mother, always very observant, said, "Have some more pancakes, Jeff."

"No, ma'am, I've got plenty."

"Why, you *never* have enough of my pancakes! Are you feeling sick?"

"No, Mrs. Carter," Jeff mumbled. "Just not very hungry, I guess. They're real good—like always."

Dan Carter studied the boy, then let his eyes run around the table. "Ed Rayburn came by last night," he said. "He brought the paper from Lexington. A couple of days old now, but I've been studying it."

Mary Carter seemed to catch a note in her husband's voice and looked at him quickly. "What does it say about the war, Dan?"

"It says here that General Pope didn't do so well against the Confederates. He got whipped pretty bad. He claimed he was going to go down and win the war right off. But he didn't do it."

Jeff's face flushed, and he flared out, "We'll see about that! He'll have to settle it with Marse Robert first." General Robert E. Lee was commander of the Confederate Army of Northern Virginia. "There have been other generals who have tried to whip him and Stonewall."

"That may be so," Dan said agreeably. With so many neighbors on both sides of the war issue, it was hard to keep a balance. There had been no better neighbors than Nelson Majors and his family, and Dan was determined now to avoid an argument with Jeff. "One thing I know is that I've got to

26

get on down the road. Those boys will be needing all kinds of things when they head South again."

"You're not fit to go. You're not well, Dan."

Dan Carter shook his head slowly in response to his wife's plea, "A man has to do what he thinks is right. I think God's told me to be all that I can to our soldier boys, and we have to obey God. That's what the Bible says."

Jeff looked up quickly. He loved Dan Carter and respected him as much as a boy could. Still, the war had somehow divided them. He said little during the talk that followed and tried to slip away as soon as he could.

Sarah caught him at the door. "Are you and Leah going fishing today, Jeff?"

"Not today."

"Why, Jeff, I never knew you to turn down a chance to go fishing!"

"Just not in the mood, I reckon."

Sarah stared at him strangely. "You sure you're feeling all right, Jeff?"

"I'm all right. Don't fuss over me!" He turned and left the house, his back stiff and his face set.

As Leah and Sarah were washing the dishes, Sarah mentioned Jeff. "I guess he's sad to have to go back. He was real short with me just now."

"He's not feeling well."

"I think he's angry, Leah. Did you two have a fight?"

Leah kept her eyes down. "He was mad because I went hunting for birds' eggs with Ezra."

"Oh, I see."

27

Leah looked up with grief in her eyes. "I didn't mean to hurt his feelings, Sarah," she protested. "I didn't think he'd be back in time to go, so I just went with Ezra."

"I see."

Catching an odd note in her sister's voice, Leah glanced at her. "Was I wrong?"

"No, Leah, but you ought to see Jeff's side of things. Boys are funny sometimes."

"They sure are!"

Sarah smiled and washed another dish. "But so are girls," she added quietly.

Leah looked miserable. She dried the plate in her hand, put it on the shelf without speaking, then complained, "I don't want to be quarreling with Jeff. He's my best friend."

"Try to make up with him," Sarah urged gently. "He might be gone for a long time. You never know what's going to happen when there's war." Her voice caught at the end, and Leah knew she was thinking, *Will I ever see Tom again?*

Leah glanced at her sister. "You're thinking about Tom, aren't you?" Her entire family knew how Sarah felt about Tom, even though she didn't talk much about him.

"I guess I was—a little," Sarah admitted. "I get so afraid for him sometimes, Leah!"

"I know, Sarah. But he'll come back when the war's over." She saw her sister's somber expression, quickly returned the last cup to the shelf, and gave her a quick hug. Then she turned and left the house for her outdoor chores, which included feeding the chickens.

She scooped a small sackful of feed from the barrel just inside the barn, crossed to the hen yard, and began to scatter it in a wide arc as she walked, calling, "Chick, chick, chick!"

The chickens came running from all directions, clucking loudly and gathering around her feet. They pecked vigorously at the feed.

Leah was startled when a voice said, "You look like you're floating in a sea of chickens, Leah."

Looking up, she saw that Ezra had come to watch. He stood there with an ax in his hand, his face wet with sweat from chopping wood.

"Seems a shame to have to chop wood, seeing it's as hot as it is," she said.

"I always say wood heats you up twice. Once when you chop it, then again when you burn it. You'll like it pretty well when winter comes."

Leah giggled. "I never thought of it that way before."

Ezra waded carefully through the sea of chickens that scolded at him. A big rooster lunged at his feet, pecking and squawking angrily. Ezra hooked its plump body under one boot toe and tossed it harmlessly into the crowd of hens. "Go take care of your women, rooster!"

He stopped in front of Leah and looked at her with a thoughtful expression. "I've been wanting to talk to you."

"About what, Ezra?"

"About Jeff."

"I don't want to talk about him. He's an old sorehead!" She flung a handful of seed hard against the henhouse.

Ezra shook his head. "That's no way for you to talk. How many times have you told me that you two have been best friends since you were kids?"

"Well, we were. But why does he have to be so . . . so. . . ."

Ezra reached into her bag and pulled out a handful of feed. He began scattering it, watching as the multicolored chickens scrambled in the dust, fighting each other. Turning to her, he said, "I guess all of us act a little bad sometimes, Leah. I know I do. Don't hold it against Jeff."

Ezra's honesty brought a flush to Leah's face, but it didn't erase her hurt feelings. She shook her head stubbornly. "He's got to learn how to behave around young ladies. He's behaving like a child."

He said suddenly, "If it hadn't been for you, I'd probably be back in a prison camp or maybe even dead. I was pretty sick."

"It wasn't much, Ezra."

"Yes, it was. I'll never forget that, Leah."

She looked at him swiftly. She had wondered at times if she had done the right thing—helping a Union soldier to escape and then involving a Confederate drummer boy, Jeff, in the plot. But now, looking at Ezra and seeing the happy contentment on his face and seeing how much he had already recovered from his devastating illness, she knew she had. "I didn't do all that much," she said.

"Yes, you did." Ezra nodded. "I owe you a lot, but I still think you ought to be a little more understanding about Jeff. A best friend is hard to find—or replace."

"He doesn't have to be so mean!"

"Jeff's got a hard row to hoe."

"So do Royal and Tom. But they don't act like soreheads! Jeff could be nice, at least."

"He's not happy, Leah, and being here he doesn't even have the war to keep his mind off what's troubling him." Ezra took some more feed and scattered it. "He's got to go back to the war. All he sees is that I'll be here enjoying the farm and being with you."

"He doesn't care about that."

"You're wrong there, Leah," Ezra said mildly. "He's jealous."

"Jealous?" Leah shot him an astonished glance. "Why, he doesn't like me that much!"

Ezra shook his head. "He sure does. I think you ought to be a little nicer to him, Leah. He's leaving tomorrow, isn't he?"

"Yes, but he's got to apologize before I give in to him," she said firmly. She finished feeding the chickens, shook the last few kernels out of the sack, left the hen yard, and waved the sack in a bright farewell to Ezra, who hefted his ax and headed back to the woodlot.

All day she thought about what Ezra had said. Finally she was all set to forgive and forget, just as soon as Jeff came and apologized, as any reasonable, civilized boy should. The day wore on, however, with no sign of Jeff. Leah watched the sun dip below the tree line and sighed. *Men!*

Matthew Henderson came for supper. He was a short, round young man whose earnest face clearly showed the crush he had on Sarah. He never would have been so bold as to try for Sarah before the war; but when Tom left, he figured he wouldn't get a better chance. Not every man went off to war—people such as Matt, who ran his father's sawmill, had to stay at home to keep up supplies.

Leah whispered to Ezra, "He's trying to court Sarah. He's been sweet on her for a long time."

"Does she like him?" Ezra whispered back.

"No, not really. All she can think about is Tom Majors." Leah shook her head. "He better go on back home. Matt Henderson's wasting his time with Sarah."

After supper, Henderson managed to persuade Sarah to go for a walk. Leah watched the two step off the porch and into the evening shadows and scoffed to Ezra, "Sarah's too polite. You wouldn't catch me walking in the moonlight with some boy I wasn't sweet on. Sarah may call me rude, but at least I don't let my manners lead some fool boy on!"

Sarah soon regretted her kindness, for Matt paused halfway down the path to the creek, quickly grasped both her hands, and pulled her toward him for a kiss.

She drew back and pushed him away. "Don't do that, Matthew Henderson!"

"Why not? You know how I feel about you," Matt protested. "I want to marry you."

"No, Matt, that's out of the question. I just don't care for you like that."

Matt argued, "My ma and pa didn't hardly know each other before they were hitched, and they learned to care for each other. We can too. You just gotta put your mind to it. You know I'll be good to you." He stared at her accusingly. "I know what's wrong with you. You're in love with that Tom Majors."

"I don't want to talk about it."

"Sarah, that won't do any good." Matt shook his head. "Look at it like this—if the North loses, which it won't, that would be a whole new country

32

in Virginia, and Tom would want to live there, not back here in Kentucky. But Kentucky—this is your home. You can't go chasing off after him and leave your whole family and friends. The South is going to lose eventually. Then what would it be like if you were married to Tom? You think any Confederate veteran's going to get fair treatment? Besides that, you've got a brother in the Union army. What if something happens to Royal? You'd blame Tom for it."

"I don't want to talk about it, Matt!" Sarah said abruptly. She didn't need Matthew Henderson telling her what she had already agonized over many nights.

Sarah whirled around on the path and almost ran back to the house.

Matt followed more slowly, and she heard him talking with her parents for a few minutes on the porch before he bade them good night and set off for home.

Later, as Sarah and Leah cleaned the kitchen and filled the woodbox for early morning baking, apparently Leah couldn't resist asking about Matt. "I guess he wanted to come courting, didn't he?"

"Oh, I suppose so, but I'm not interested in that." Sarah deliberately turned away and began to vigorously scrub the already spotless counter.

"I sure wish I had one boy I was sweet on and another sweet on me. You sure are lucky, Sarah. Are you going to hold out and marry Tom when the war's over?"

Sarah grew flustered. "It's too soon to talk about things like that. I don't know—the war may go on for another five years."

"It can't last that long," Leah protested with the innocence of youth.

"I just don't know. Don't pester me about it, Leah."

Later, at evening Bible reading, Dan noticed that his oldest daughter was moody, but he decided to let her work it out on her own. After he had read from Scripture and explained what he thought it meant, he closed the big, old family Bible and began to talk about his plans.

"I've made up my mind to go again," he said quietly. "I know I'm not in the best of health, but God and Leah will go with me."

"I'll take care of you, Pa," Leah said. "We'll get along."

"I really don't think you should go this time, Dan," Mrs. Carter protested. "You had a bad spell two weeks ago. Suppose you have one while you're out in the camp?"

"I'd take care of him, Ma," Leah repeated. "He's had them before when we've been out, and we did just fine."

"You're a fine young woman, Leah," her mother said. "You do very well with cooking and caring for your father, but there's things only your father can do. And I worry about you too, a young girl in those rough camps with all those soldiers."

The family discussion went back and forth. Jeff took no part in it but sat leaning against the wall, his chair tilted back. He himself felt Mr. Carter was making a mistake, but he was not really family, and he sure didn't feel like chiming in on their affairs tonight. He kept watching Leah, stealing glances at her. Once their eyes met, but they both glanced away quickly.

"Well, I've never tried to tell you what to do, Dan," Mrs. Carter said. "That's not a wife's place, but this time I think it would be foolish for you to go. You're just not able. You're not as strong now as you were the last time you went out, and you struggled the whole time."

"I'll go with them, Mrs. Carter."

Every eye turned on Ezra, who, like Jeff, had remained silent until now. He added quickly, "I can do the driving and cut the wood, and even bargain with the soldiers. All Mr. Carter will have to do is order me and Leah around and do his preaching."

"Why, you can't do that, Ezra," Leah interrupted. "We're counting on you to keep the farm up and watch Mother and Sarah."

"I surely would feel better, knowing Ezra was helping you, Dan." Mrs. Carter's voice brightened. "And you said Ray Studdard was looking for extra work. You were going to hire him before Ezra came."

"I was hoping that with Ezra I wouldn't have to dip into our savings to pay Ray . . . but I could use Ezra's help on the way . . . and Ray is a good hand." He nodded. "Are you sure you want to go, Ezra?"

"I guess this Mr. Studdard can take care of the farm. Not as good as I could." Ezra grinned. He turned to Mr. Carter and said, "I'd really like to go. It would give me a chance to show how much I appreciate what you've done for me."

Mrs. Carter broke in. "If you've got to go, Dan, I insist you take Ezra with you. If you do need help, he'll be there. Between the two of them, Ezra and Leah can make things about as good as they can be on a journey like that."

In the end the Carters all agreed. Ezra would go along with Dan and Leah. The three would have the best supply and Bible preaching business around.

Dan smiled at his helpers. "Well, looks like I'm just going to be taken care of like a king."

Leah went over and hugged him. "You deserve it, Pa. You just sit back and tell Ezra and me what to do, and we'll take care of you."

No one seemed to notice that Jeff had said nothing during the entire discussion and that the scowl on his face had deepened with each passing minute.

Later he silently climbed the ladder to the attic room he bunked in. In slow motion he stripped to his underwear and collapsed on the narrow cot under the eaves. For hours he lay awake, staring out the single window at the full moon. No one heard his quiet plea, "If You're there, God, why don't You help me like You do Mr. Carter?"

Jeff would have given almost anything to be the one to travel with Dan and Leah—without Ezra. But he wouldn't give up his loyalty to his father, and that meant returning to the army with the supplies. Life just wasn't fair, and God didn't seem to care about the Majors family as He did about the Carters.

The next morning at breakfast Jeff announced that he was leaving immediately to rejoin his father. His wagon was hitched to the front porch, and his mules were fed and watered.

"Jeff, it's Sunday. Please go to church with us

first," urged Dan. "It's your last chance to say good-bye to your old neighbors."

"No, sir, thank you just the same. I need to get an early start," Jeff replied without quite meeting the older man's gaze. "I'm thanking you, and my father is too, for all you've done for Esther and for us, but I've got to go."

"Why, it can't make that much difference in your travel time, son," Mrs. Carter urged. "And you don't know when you'll get as fiery a sermon as you will from Preacher Edwards."

"Thanks, Mr. and Mrs. Carter, but I'll just be on my way."

A few minutes later Jeff brought his bedroll and pack down from the attic and threw them behind the wagon seat. The wagonload of corn, oats, and salt pork would make a big difference to the troops.

He and Leah had helped Ezra escape by offering to go after supplies and then hiding him under the tarp in the wagon with the furs the soldiers had collected for trading. Sometimes he wished he'd never given in to Leah and helped Ezra, but at least his father's troops would get the benefit.

He said good-bye to everyone, nodding to Leah and mumbling an emotionless "Good-bye, Leah" to her. He climbed up on the seat and barked out the order for his mules to move out. He'd not gotten far, however, when he heard a voice calling. He slowed and looked back to see Leah run up beside the wagon. "Whoa!" he said, and the mules drew to an abrupt halt.

"I just wanted to really say good-bye." Leah looked up at Jeff nervously. "I wish you didn't have to go." She half raised her hand toward him, then let it drop to her side.

Jeff's hurt erupted in his voice. "You've already said that, and so have I. We just don't get what we want sometimes, do we?"

Leah bit her lip, for his tone was curt. "Jeff, don't be so mean to me."

"Mean? I'm not mean!"

Jeff didn't know if he wanted to be mean or sorry, but somehow it seemed easier to be mean. He'd always been proud, hating to admit he was wrong; and now he wanted more than anything to get off the wagon and take her hands and tell her he'd been wrong and foolish, but somehow he couldn't do it.

"It . . . might be a long time before you come back," Leah half whispered.

"I'll be all right."

"You can't know that. Anyone can get hurt in a battle."

"Don't worry about it," Jeff muttered.

Leah seemed fully aware that her entire family, and Ezra too, were watching from the yard. If they had been alone, he thought she might have reached out and taken his arm and said what was in her heart. She, too, must be sorry and hating the argument that they'd had.

But people were watching, and he figured she couldn't bring herself to be the first to give in, in front of them. She didn't say more than, "Well, I hope you have a safe trip." Then she turned and walked away, her face stiff.

Jeff stared at her straight back, fought the urge to jump down and run after her, and instead turned angrily around, gritted his teeth, and yelled, "Git up!"

The mules, startled as much by his jerk on the reins as by his shout, jumped forward into their harnesses, abruptly pulling the heavy wagon into the lane.

As they finally rounded the bend and the house faded away behind the trees, Jeff slammed his fist against the wagon seat, frustrated and angry. "Why do I have to be such a stubborn, no-account fool!"

3

Jeff Makes Another Mistake

The trip back to Virginia seemed to last forever. Jeff had no trouble getting through the lines; his permit from the Richmond quartermaster paved the way just as it had when he and Leah had traveled the opposite direction with Ezra. But despite the good weather and the bright, sunlit countryside, his heart seemed to grow heavier as he drew closer to his new Virginia home.

At night when he stopped at farmhouses and traded a little of his grain supply for a hot meal and a barn roof to sleep under, everyone talked about how Lee had whipped Pope. When they discovered that Jeff was a member of the Confederate army, though only a drummer boy, they plied him with questions as if he were an expert. And when they found out his supplies were for "their boys in gray," most returned the small grain payment he had made to them.

Jeff actually knew little more than the farmers and ended each conversation with "We'll just have to whip them, same as we did before."

He arrived in Richmond on Saturday afternoon, the twenty-third day of August.

When he pulled up in front of the quartermaster's, the young lieutenant who'd issued him his pass came out to greet him. Looking at the heaping load of feed, he smiled, saying, "Well, you did come back. What happened to the girl who was with you?"

Jeff hesitated, then said simply, "She's staying with her family for a while."

"Well, we can use this feed." The lieutenant nodded. "After you get unloaded, come to my office, and I'll see you get paid for it."

Jeff did what the lieutenant said, and later, as he took the Confederate currency from the officer, he said to himself, *Mr. Carter'll be glad to see this. It'll help pay for having that neighbor in to work when he leaves with Leah and Ezra.* Aloud he said, "What's happening with the army? My pa's an officer in the Stonewall Brigade."

"They're getting ready for the next fight," the lieutenant replied. He leaned back in his chair and shook his head. "General Lee doesn't say much bad about anybody, but he sure gets his dander up sometimes about those bluecoats!"

"Where's it going to be?" Jeff inquired.

"Don't know. But General Lee sure did make a monkey out of Pope! That Pope, he made all kinds of boasts about how he's going to whip General Lee. He said anybody caught helping us Rebels will be treated as a spy. Did you ever hear of such a thing?" He grinned. "General Lee just drawled that fancy talk he has and said Pope must be 'suppressed.' I said a lot worse words, myself! But I guess we'll whip those Yankees. Just like we did last time."

After his wagon was emptied, Jeff took his leave of the lieutenant. Knowing he couldn't catch up with the army that night, he decided to pay a visit to Silas Carter, Dan's uncle, who lived just outside Richmond.

He climbed into the empty wagon and drove down the main street.

Richmond was still a beehive of activity. The city contained the only Confederate factory set up to manufacture arms, the Tredagar Iron Works, and smoke poured out of its chimney night and day, even on Sundays. The Richmond streets were packed with soldiers—officers and enlisted men— as well as what seemed to be thousands of civilians.

Richmond was the heart of the Confederacy. He'd heard talk reported by the Northern newspapers that the Union troops were threatening, "On to Richmond!" and General McClellan had promised to take the city for the North. He had failed, however, at the Battles of the Seven Days, and now was planning another attempt.

Silas Carter's house was five miles outside of town. Jeff had visited Leah there often over the previous year, when she and Sarah had spent several months caring for their elderly uncle, whose health was much worse than their father's. After Sarah had left abruptly, accused by a Confederate officer of spying for the North, Jeff and Leah had spent hours talking and laughing as they cared for Uncle Silas's farm. It was there that she had discovered Ezra Payne, who had escaped the disease-filled Confederate prison camp outside town.

As Jeff drew near Uncle Silas's house, he thought again of the quarrel he'd had with Leah and muttered, "She sure is stubborn, that girl is!" And he remembered it was that same stubbornness that had finally convinced him to help her rescue Ezra and get him to her family in Kentucky in the first place. Pulling up in front of the house, he leaped out, tied the team to the hitching post, took the porch steps two at a time, and knocked smartly on the door.

It opened almost at once.

"Why, Jeff! Come in the house, boy. I didn't know you were back."

"Good to see you again, Mr. Carter." Jeff smiled and shook his hand. It startled him how much alike Silas and his nephew Dan were getting to look, especially now that Dan's hair was turning gray.

Silas was older, with a white beard and a headful of silvery hair. There was a smile on his lips as he pulled Jeff inside. "Come in, boy, and tell me what all has been going on. How's my Kentucky family doing? I've been sort of concerned about you too. That's a long haul for a young feller. Sit down there at the table and tie into some of this cornbread and beans. There's plenty. I want to hear about how you three got away."

"Why, I wrote you about it, Mr. Carter, as soon as I got to Kentucky."

"Oh, sure, but hearing about something is better than reading about it, don't you think?"

"Yes, I guess it is." Despite his new resentment of Ezra, Jeff remembered with pride and pleasure how they had sneaked him through the lines and made it all the way to the Carters' farm in Kentucky without a hitch.

"Sit down, boy," Silas insisted, and soon Jeff was eating the sweet cornbread and smoky beans that Silas made so well, washing them down with cool buttermilk.

Jeff was glad to see Silas again. He'd grown fond of him, and now he sat and watched Silas clean up the dishes and wipe the counter and table with a damp rag.

"Well, we had quite a time of it, but we made it back."

"It was Lucy Driscoll who told the soldiers about Ezra, wasn't it?"

"Yes, sir. I sure didn't think Lucy would do a thing like that."

Silas grinned suddenly. "I think she was jealous of you, Jeff."

"Jealous?" Jeff's bewildered face echoed the surprise in his voice.

"Why, sure! That little girl's always got everything she wanted. When she saw you liked Leah best, she just purely couldn't take it."

Jeff flushed and shook his head. "I dunno. Never thought of it that way."

"Well, I did. But go on with the story."

"Not much to it. I rode hard and got ahead of the patrol they sent out to catch Ezra."

"Guess you had to ride pretty hard." Silas had once said he liked the way Jeff never boasted but just considered himself an ordinary boy who did what he had to.

"Sure did. Had to ride *around* the patrol. Only got there a few minutes before they did."

"If they'd caught Ezra, he'd have been sent back to prison camp. He surely would've died there. Where'd you hide him?"

"Oh, I just told him to take my horse on ahead. He was out of sight before the patrol pulled up."

"You saved his bacon, Jeff—and Leah's too, if they'd found out her part in it."

"Don't know about that, sir."

"If they'd caught her with an escaped Federal prisoner, she'd have been in real trouble."

"When they found out my father was an officer in the Stonewall Brigade, and that I was the drummer boy, they didn't waste any more time."

44

"Things went all right the rest of the way?"

"Yes, sir. They went fine," Jeff answered. Getting fed up with Leah and all the time she spent with Ezra didn't really count as trouble, he guessed.

"Here, have some more cornbread. I know how much you like it."

Soon Jeff was spooning the last crumbs of cornbread soaked in rich buttermilk out of his cup—a treat he had enjoyed often at Silas's home.

"That sure was good!" He sighed with satisfaction. "You make the best cornbread I know of."

Silas shrugged, replying with a modest grin, "Anybody can make good cornbread, if they've a mind to." He leaned back in his cane chair, stared at the boy, and noted with pride, "Looks to me like you're kind of a hero, Jeff, the way you saved Leah and Ezra."

Jeff shifted uneasily in his chair, reached out, and pulled the bowl containing blackberry cobbler toward him. He took a bite and shook his head. "I don't reckon I'm any kind of a hero. I didn't want Leah to get caught, is all."

"Well, you sure saved her neck and that young fella Ezra too. I know he's grateful to you."

"Don't know about that." Jeff cut himself off before he said anything unkind about Ezra. He had no reason to, not really, even though he included him in his lingering anger at Leah.

Jeff's discomfort seemed to puzzle Silas. "They're all right, aren't they—the folks back in Kentucky? I sure think a lot of that nephew of mine, Dan. How's he doing? You're not keeping anything back, are you, son?"

"No, sir. There's nothing wrong with anybody. Mr. Carter's about the same—not too well but doing well enough, like always," Jeff answered slowly, taking another bite of cobbler. "He's going to follow the Union army as a sutler again."

"That's pretty hard work. A sick man doesn't have any business doing a thing like that." Silas's concern for his nephew was plain on his weather-beaten face.

"That's what Mrs. Carter says, but Mr. Carter says that God's told him to do it, so he's going to do it. When Mr. Carter gets something in his head, he doesn't change his mind just because he doesn't feel very sprightly."

Silas chuckled. "That sounds like Dan, all right. He always was a strong Christian. Stronger than me, I think. How's the rest of the family? How's that little sister of yours?"

Jeff spent the next hour telling about life on the farm in Pineville.

Silas Carter sat back and listened. Finally when Jeff came to the end of his story, Silas said, "You're not talking much about Leah, Jeff. Time was, your best friend and your escapades with her used up almost all your talkin' time."

"Not much to say," Jeff replied shortly.

"You sound like you're put out with her."

Jeff suddenly nodded. "Well, I am, to tell the truth. I don't mess in other people's business, Mr. Carter, but I think she's making a big mistake. Maybe all of them are."

Silas leaned forward, his bright blue eyes fixed on Jeff. "This have something to do with Ezra?"

Jeff felt himself flush, but he kept his head high. In for a penny, in for a pound. He wouldn't clam up now. "Yes, it does! They've taken him in like he's family, and he's nothing but a Yankee."

"Well, their son, Royal, he's a Yankee too. He's in the Union army."

"Well, *Ezra* ain't their son," Jeff snapped. "And besides—" He broke off and bit his lip angrily.

"What is it, Jeff? You don't like Ezra just because he's a Yankee? Is there something else?"

Jeff was flustered. He said finally, "I think Leah's making too much of him. She's too young to be interested in boys like that. She doesn't know how Ezra might be feeling toward her."

"Well, they're pretty good friends, but you two have been friends a lot longer. Are you feeling a different way toward her now too?"

"I told her we went back a lot further than her and Ezra," Jeff said eagerly. "But she wouldn't even go fishing with me. She was out hunting birds' eggs with him. That's what we always did together. If she wanted someone to go hunting birds' eggs with her, why didn't she ask me?"

"I don't know. Why didn't she? Maybe you were busy."

Jeff remembered how he'd insisted on going off to hunt rabbits by himself, and he gnawed his lip in a worried fashion. "She could have asked me," he said stubbornly.

Silas, perhaps figuring he'd gotten about as much out of the young man as he was going to during this conversation, merely responded, "You'll work it out, Jeff. You two always have. Now pay for your supper by chopping me some wood!"

Later, at the window, as he watched Jeff swinging the ax with a vengeance under the old oak tree, Silas said to himself, *That boy's got himself tangled up in his own harness. I don't think I can talk to him right now. When a boy's stubborn like that, he's got to get himself out of it.*

Jeff was tired and knew he could spend the night with Silas without having to do anything else, but he also knew the old man appreciated any help he got. There were plenty of chores to be done, and he worked hard for the rest of the day.

Late that afternoon he took a break, slumped down on the dirt by the front porch, and then looked up when he heard the jingle of harness and whisper of wheels spinning down the road. A familiar buggy was approaching.

It stopped in front of the house.

He scrambled to his feet and wiped his sweaty face on his sleeve as Lucy Driscoll jumped down and ran toward him.

Her voice nearly screeched his name. "Jeff! Jeff!" She launched herself toward him and grabbed him around the neck.

"Hello, Lucy," Jeff said awkwardly as he untangled her arms and set her away from his dusty, sweat-soaked clothes. He still disliked the girl. She had always treated Leah badly. Just because Leah's family wasn't like hers—Lucy's parents were two of the most important social leaders in the Richmond area—didn't mean Lucy could treat her like trash.

Lucy Driscoll was a pretty girl, small and well-shaped, with blonde hair and blue eyes. Her father was a prominent, wealthy planter.

Lucy saw Jeff's frown and bit her lip. "When the lieutenant told me you were back, I just couldn't wait to talk to you, Jeff," she said timidly.

"About what?" he responded roughly. It was not Lucy's social snub of Leah that disturbed him the most. What seemed unforgivable was that Lucy had informed Captain Wesley Lyons that Leah was trying to sneak away with an escaped prisoner. It had been Lucy's spite that had almost gotten Leah and Ezra captured. Jeff and Leah had talked a lot about Lucy's betrayal, and neither of them had any warm feelings for the girl. He looked at her sternly.

Lucy looked down at the ground. "You're mad at me, aren't you, Jeff?"

"Don't know why you should think that," Jeff said shortly.

Lucy looked up, and Jeff saw how worry creased her forehead. Her eyes almost teared. Her lips were trembling. "I was wrong to do what I did," she offered as she plucked hesitantly at his sleeve. She waited, and when he didn't speak she added, "I shouldn't have told on Leah like I did. It was wrong of me. Friends should be loyal."

Ordinarily, Jeff would have been quick to accept the girl's apology. However, his feelings had been rubbed raw with his quarrel with Leah, and he wasn't in the mood to forgive any girl anything right now.

"You *never* were nice to Leah," he accused. "You made fun of her clothes and the way she acted at your party. You snubbed her on the street. You turned your friends against her. You even tried to get me mad at her."

"I know, and I was wrong. Mama told me I was. I guess that's why I was so mad. But I didn't want to see Leah get hurt—really, I didn't, Jeff! I thought it would be better if she were stopped before that bad Yankee—you know—tried to take advantage of her!"

"Ezra wouldn't be anything but a gentleman to her. And besides, you know what would've happened if that patrol had caught her with Ezra? She could have been arrested as a spy and hanged or shot. How's that better for her?"

"Oh, no, our boys wouldn't dare hurt a Southern lady!"

"That's what they do with spies," Jeff said roughly. "Male or female, Northern or Southern. How would you have liked that?"

Lucy's lips began to tremble again and tears formed in each eye. "I'm sorry," she whispered. "I know I behave so badly sometimes. But I just don't have any worldly experience, not like you and Leah. I truly wouldn't want anything bad to happen to Leah."

Jeff was tempted to give her some sort of assurance, but his stubborn streak won out. "Well," he declared, "you sure have a funny way of showing it! You could get somebody killed, Lucy."

He walked away without another word.

Lucy stared after him. Then turning slowly, she walked back to the buggy where her father's most trusted slave sat holding the reins, watching carefully for her safety.

When she got in, she motioned brusquely and commanded, "Go on, Sam."

He spoke gently to the horses and turned them toward home. As the team plodded along, he spoke with determination. "That young man ain't got no manners, Miss Lucy. You stay away from him!"

Lucy whispered, "No, he's right, Sam." She had hoped that Jeff would forgive her, but his harsh response had crushed her, and she huddled in the seat as the buggy rolled down the road.

After supper that night Silas said, "I saw Lucy Driscoll stop and talk to you this afternoon."

Jeff frowned. "Yes, she did. Fool girl! I guess I told her off!"

Silas shot a quick look at him. "What did she say?"

"Oh, she said she was sorry about the way she told on Leah and Ezra. A lot of good that would have done if they had gotten caught! She's nothing but a little brat!"

Silas wrinkled his forehead and leaned back in his chair. He said mildly, "Good that you've never done anything wrong, Jeff."

Jeff looked up suddenly, and when he saw the old man's eyes on him, he flushed. "Why, I've done my share of wrong things," he protested.

"Nobody ever forgave you for them, I don't suppose?" Silas asked.

"Why, sure," Jeff floundered. "I mean, of course they did!" He was nervous and uncomfortable. Making a mistake was sure different from putting someone's life in danger because you're a fool! Finally, after a long silence, he cleared his throat. "I guess you think I was too hard on Lucy?"

"The Bible says if we hold a grudge against anyone, we're wrong. Lucy was wrong to do what she did, but she was right to feel bad about it—and right to ask you to forgive her."

Jeff shifted uneasily in his chair. "Well, I didn't think about that."

The old man said nothing.

Jeff finally blurted out, "I guess I was wrong too, wasn't I?"

"You have to decide that, Jeff. It's not up to me. God has a way of making us feel pretty bad when we do wrong things. It's what the preachers call 'conviction.' If I were you, I'd think about it, though. Next time it may be you that needs forgiving."

Jeff was troubled, and as they washed the dishes, the two of them talked earnestly about everything except Lucy and the way Jeff had treated her. At last Jeff said, "Well, I was wrong, Mr. Carter—I sure was. I'll just have to swallow my pride and tell her so."

"I know one way you can do that."

"How's that, sir?"

"Well, it's Sunday tomorrow. We can go to church in the morning. The Driscolls are always there. It'd be a good chance for you, after the service, to make it right with her."

Jeff nodded slowly. "All right, that's what I'll do then." He looked at Silas and shook his head. "It sure is hard to say sorry, isn't it?"

"I guess it is. The hardest thing a person has to say is 'I was wrong' and 'I'm sorry.'" Silas grinned at him. "But after you say it, you'll feel good, boy. Wait and see if you don't."

Jeff knew that Silas Carter was right, but his stubborn streak still gave him problems. That night as he lay in bed, he thought a long time about the next day.

Wonder why it's so hard to say you're sorry? Ought to be easy—but it never is!

4

Jeff Makes a New Friend

Jeff felt uncomfortable entering the large, white-frame Baptist church set back from the main road. He arrived with Silas Carter just as the service was beginning.

"I guess we're a little bit late," Silas said as they got out of the buggy. He tied up his farm horses, curried to a shine and wearing their matching "dress up" harnesses, then joined Jeff at the top of the steps. "We're here for the preaching though, and that's my favorite part anyhow."

Jeff looked around uncomfortably. "I'm not really dressed for church. I wish I could've gone back to camp and at least got my uniform."

"Well, what you're like on the outside don't really matter that much," Silas said. He winked at Jeff, and a smile touched his lips. "The preacher said once that some come to eye the clothes, and some come to close their eyes!" He laughed at the old joke and then shrugged. "This isn't a real fancy church anyhow. We're mostly farm folks here. Come on, Jeff. Maybe we can get a seat up front."

Jeff would have preferred a seat in the very back row or even in the balcony, if the church had one.

As they made their way down a side aisle, he glanced over his shoulder and saw that there was a balcony and that it was almost filled with the slaves who had brought their children and come with their masters. The main part of the church was fairly crowded and already beginning to warm up.

Jeff looked quickly over the congregation and saw only one person he knew. Cecil Taylor was sitting a third of the way from the front. Cecil was the same age as Jeff, fifteen. The two of them had met at Lucy Driscoll's birthday party. Cecil was a thin boy with chestnut hair and bright blue eyes. He looked surprised when he saw Jeff and winked at him as he passed by.

"Here—this is a good seat," Silas announced loudly. He was hard of hearing and didn't know that his voice carried almost over the singing.

Jeff slipped in beside him and scrunched down, hoping no one would pay attention.

"Got plenty of room, Jeff?" Silas demanded, just as loudly.

"Yes, sir," Jeff whispered.

"Good." Silas looked around and said with satisfaction, "Always like to get a good seat up front, don't you?"

"Yes, sir," Jeff mumbled.

"Here, we can share this songbook. Let's hear you sing out, boy! I love these old songs!"

The congregation was singing "Amazing Grace," a song Jeff was thankful he knew very well. It was one of Stonewall Jackson's favorites, and the general insisted on the troops' singing it at every service. Jeff knew the words and sang along while helping to hold the book for Silas.

When the song was finished, the song leader, a tall thin man with a head of bushy black hair, said, "Fine singing—very fine! Now let's sing ol' Hundred."

Jeff didn't know the name, but he recognized the song as the congregation vigorously joined in:

"Praise God from whom all blessings flow,
Praise Him all creatures here below,
Praise Him above, ye heavenly host,
Praise Father, Son, and Holy Ghost."

From time to time Silas would smile at Jeff, saying, "Sing out, Jeff! God gave you a good pair of lungs."

"Yes, sir, I will," Jeff always responded, hoping people wouldn't get too annoyed at the old man's somewhat disruptive enthusiasm.

Halfway through the song service, Jeff spotted Lucy, sitting with her parents. They were to his right, and her eyes met his. He saw that her face was pale, and she looked very serious.

She makes me feel like a sheep-killing dog, he thought. *I didn't have any business taking off on her like I did.* He continued to hold the songbook, but all during the singing he was practicing his speech of apology.

Then a tall, heavily built man got to his feet. He wore a black suit, a white shirt, and a heavy gold chain that glinted in the light as he walked. Jeff knew he was imagining things, but he felt there was as much power in this man's voice as in his body.

"We're delighted to have you here this morning. Those of you who are not of our particular flock, we welcome you especially. The good Christians of Richmond are pleased to open our place of worship to the many visitors we seem to be attracting during this time of trouble in our land."

"That's Preacher Jones, Tyronzo Jones," Silas explained to Jeff. "He sure do know how to preach the Word. Wait'll he gets going."

Jeff slouched a little lower in his seat as the lady on the other side of him glared at Silas's interruption.

Preacher Jones welcomed the visitors, exhorting them all to come back, then made a few announcements about the upcoming church picnic, the ladies' relief society meeting, and the choir's new fall practice schedule. Then he cleared his throat and announced, "We'll take a special collection this morning. It'll go for food and medicine for our brave soldiers who are in the hospitals here in Richmond. I exhort you to give liberally."

A wooden collection plate soon came by, and Jeff reached into his pocket and pulled out several of the bills he had gotten from the lieutenant the previous day. He felt Silas nudge him and heard him say, "It goes for a good cause, boy."

"Yes, sir, it sure does."

After the offering, Preacher Jones got up and announced that his text would be from the apostle Paul's letter to the Roman church, the tenth chapter, verses nine and ten. He read, "If thou shalt confess with thy mouth the Lord Jesus, and shalt believe in thine heart that God hath raised him from the dead, thou shalt be saved. For with the heart man believeth unto righteousness; and with the mouth confession is made unto salvation."

The preacher began his sermon soft and low. Jeff had to lean forward at first to be sure he caught every word. As the preacher warmed up, pleading with his congregation about the importance of confessing Jesus Christ as Lord, his voice rose and fell—one minute almost sobbing his compassion for poor, lost souls; the next minute shouting with joy for the marvelous gift of salvation.

"It's not enough, folks, simply to believe that Jesus is the Savior," he admonished. "You must say it aloud with your lips." His voice echoed and rattled the windows. "No man can follow Jesus silently, nor a woman either!"

Jeff listened intently to the sermon. He had never felt he was an "on fire" Christian like Dan and Silas Carter. He'd come to admire Stonewall Jackson, who made no secret at all of his belief in Jesus Christ. The general spoke publicly in meetings and privately to many individuals. Jeff remembered vividly how the great Stonewall had spoken to him and Charlie Bowers, his fellow drummer, when they first joined the brigade. The general had been pleased to talk about his faith with them and had insisted on their coming to the revival going on near their camp. He sure was brave about his faith.

Now as Preacher Jones continued to preach, Jeff thought, *It takes a lot of nerve to come right out and tell people you're a Christian. Why, I think I'd rather charge a bunch of Yankees with those new-fangled breechloaders!*

The last fiery echoes of the sermon rang more than an hour after Preacher Jones had begun so softly. His voice reverberated from the corners of the church. "The time is now! Those of you who don't know Jesus, I invite you to come—to believe in your heart that He is the Savior, to confess that fact with your lips. Come while we sing!"

As the congregation joined in singing "As We

Gather at the River," Jeff watched at least a half dozen people move down the aisle toward the front.

"Look at that, Jeff!" Silas whispered loudly. "Good to see all those sinners finding Jesus!"

Preacher Jones talked to each one of the penitent folks briefly and prayed with them, while other members came to speak with them as well. Finally he said, "These have come, taking Jesus as their Savior. We'll be counseling with them." He hesitated, shaking his head. "This is one battle, folks, you'll be glad to lose. I encourage you, do not sleep tonight without giving your life to Jesus. In these uncertain days, none of us knows how soon we'll be meeting Him. Please, please, be ready!"

After a short, deliberate pause, Preacher Jones motioned to Silas. "We will now have the benediction. I ask Mr. Silas Carter to pronounce it."

Jeff was a little startled. He knew that Silas Carter was a fine Christian, but he had no idea that he was so well thought of.

Silas prayed in his usual, firm voice, asking the blessings of God on those who had just entered the kingdom. Before he closed, he prayed for the soldiers on the field of battle about to face death.

"Both North and South," he said firmly, and Jeff felt a rustle over the congregation. "These are all the concern of Jesus Christ—Southern and Northern boys—and we pray for all of them."

There were a few "Amens" after Silas ended his prayer, and the congregation began leaving the pews.

Jeff went at once to where Lucy stood with her family. He knew he would never be able to apologize in public, although he intended to try.

Mrs. Driscoll said, "Why, it's our young friend from the Stonewall Brigade. Jeffrey, isn't it?"

"Yes, ma'am. Jeff Majors."

"Well, it's good to see you, my boy." Mr. Driscoll leaned forward and shook Jeff's hand firmly. "I understand you've been to Kentucky for supplies. We thought at first maybe you had gone with the army."

"I expect I'll leave right away to catch up with them, Mr. Driscoll. I just got back."

"Well, I insist on you and Mr. Carter having dinner with us," Mr. Driscoll said. He looked over at Silas and smiled. "We can continue the discussion we had the last time we spoke about our Lord's coming."

Silas smiled slightly. "Yes, I thought you might appreciate a little more enlightenment on that, Brother Driscoll. We'll be glad to go, won't we, Jeff?"

"Yes, sir, that would be nice."

"Well, you just follow us," Mr. Driscoll said, then turned to leave the church with his wife and Lucy.

Jeff and Silas in their buggy followed the Driscolls' carriage to their home, a large mansion two miles down the road. As they dismounted and joined the Driscolls, slaves came to take the teams away.

"Come on inside," Mr. Driscoll said jovially. "We don't cook on Sunday, but we have a mountain of food cooked up on Saturday. I hope you like cold fried chicken and potato salad, because that's what dinner is."

"Nothing better than that," Silas agreed heartily. "Isn't that right, Jeff?"

"Yes, sir!" Jeff replied with enthusiasm.

He was somewhat nervous about Lucy. She had not spoken to him at all, and he was having second thoughts about the speech he'd planned to make.

The visitors were ushered in, and soon they all sat down at a large, oval mahogany table covered with a sparkling white tablecloth. The crystal glasses caught the sunlight filtering down from the high windows. A house servant, wearing a spotless white dress, set down a huge silver tray. Removing the cover, she said, "There it is. I hopes you likes fried chicken."

The table soon was loaded down with vegetables, potato salad, pickles, three kinds of bread, and large pitchers of milk.

After Mr. Driscoll asked the blessing, he said, "Now, you two start in. I know what it's like to be starving to death after a long sermon."

Jeff put a chicken leg on his plate, and Mr. Driscoll laughed, "That's hardly enough to whet your appetite, young man. You need more than that to keep yourself growing strong!" He piled Jeff's plate high and then added, "You lay your ears back and fly right at it, Jeff."

He laughed again, turning to Silas. "Help yourself while I try to help Mr. Carter here see the light on this business he thinks he knows so much about in the book of Revelation."

Mr. Driscoll and Mr. Carter engaged in a rather lighthearted discussion of the second coming of Jesus. Actually their ideas were not greatly different, but they enjoyed arguing doctrine. Mrs. Driscoll talked incessantly to Jeff, barely giving him time to answer her questions and put away a healthy portion of all the good food.

After the meal, Mrs. Driscoll gave the two young people the chance Jeff had been waiting for.

"Lucy, why don't you go show Jeff the new fish pond you designed? I know you're proud of it, and Jeff might be interested."

"Yes, Mother." Lucy rose from her chair.

Jeff couldn't tell from her tone of voice, or her almost expressionless face, what she thought of a chance to talk to him alone. Feeling foolish and uncomfortable, he followed her from the room.

They proceeded down a long hall with a polished oak floor, out the sun room door, and along the expansive veranda to the side lawn.

Jeff tried to start the conversation on safe ground. "That was a good meal. I don't get cooking like that very often."

"Rosalee's a very good cook," Lucy answered briefly.

She led him around a pathway to the side of the house, and there under a huge oak they came to stand beside a pond that had been built of cement and stone. It was at least ten feet across, and lily pads covered some of the surface.

"Daddy had it built because he likes to watch the fish," Lucy said. "He let me design it." She was not smiling and seemed to be depressed.

Jeff looked down and caught the flash of a reddish fish. "I see one!" he cried. "Look! Right there!" He leaned over and looked down into the depths, where he saw the fish as they came toward the surface, eager for the dried food they had come to expect every time people approached.

"They sure are pretty. I've never seen pet fish before. Your father called them 'goldfish'—they look more red to me. Are they good to eat?"

"No," Lucy murmured. "They're just to look at. One of my father's fancy habits."

Jeff tried to carry on a conversation about the fish. Finally he gave up the pretense, took a deep breath, turned to Lucy, and blurted out, "Lucy, I was mean to you yesterday. I should have accepted your apology. I hope you'll accept mine. I'm sorry."

At once, Lucy, who had been staring into the water, turned to face him. Shock mingled with surprise and happiness were in her expression. "You *were* mean," she said. "But I guess I deserved it."

"Well, like Silas Carter says, I guess we all deserve a whipping sometimes—and I've done worse than what you did. So I really came to church to meet you. I really wanted to tell you I was sorry. And I am."

The sober look that had been on the girl's face had vanished. She smiled, and her eyes grew bright. "Oh, Jeff, I am sorry! I don't know what made me do such a terrible thing! I don't know what Leah must think of me."

"Well, she was put out with you, Lucy, just like I was. But like I said, we all do foolish things from time to time."

He suddenly laughed. "You know, I stayed awake last night till after midnight practicing that speech, just saying, 'Lucy, I'm sorry.' I don't know why it's so hard for us to confess we're wrong—at least it is for me."

"It is for me too," Lucy said quickly.

She made a pretty sight as she stood before him. She was wearing a bright yellow dress trimmed with light green ribbons and a matching ribbon in her hair that brought out the green highlights in her blue eyes. Her hair was the color of spun honey.

She moved close to Jeff, extended her hand until her fingertips were barely touching his chest, and pled, "Let's not ever fuss again, all right, Jeff?"

"That's fine with me, Lucy, but I just don't know if I can promise it. Folks do tell me I tend to have a quick temper," he answered with a grin. He bit his lip. "I'm such a stubborn cuss—always getting my foot in my mouth. I'd like to promise, but all I can say is I'll do my best."

Lucy laughed. "That might be a description of me," she answered. "I'm always getting in trouble. Daddy spoils me frightfully and doesn't even seem to know it." She smiled, her cheeks dimpling slightly. "Of course, I let him do it."

"I don't blame you a bit," Jeff said cheerfully. "I wish somebody'd spoil me! I'd take all that I could get."

Lucy moved closer. "I'm so glad you came! Now we can be friends, can't we?"

Jeff stared at her with surprise. "Sure we can. Of course, I'm hardly ever around here. I'll be leaving to catch up with the Stonewall Brigade— probably right away."

"I know, but you'll be coming back. And when you do, I'll be waiting. I'll have another party, and you can come and bring anybody you want to. If Leah comes back, she can come too, and I'll be very nice to her, to make up for last time."

"That'd be real good, Lucy."

Jeff was amazed to discover how pleased it made him feel to forgive Lucy—it had taken away all his ill-will toward this girl. Although he knew it was he himself who had changed, it was like she was a different girl too.

When he and Silas got in the buggy and started for home, he commented to the older man, "You know, she's not a bad girl at all, Lucy Driscoll. She just made a mistake."

Silas looked at him. "I guess we all do that, as I've said so often. She's a fine young lady. Spoiled a little bit, but no wonder, as pretty as she is and coming from a fine home like that. It'd be a wonder if she wasn't."

They talked as the horses trotted down the road, the dust rising behind them in a lazy spiral. Jeff thought about the day, took a deep breath, and said, "I wish I could get out of every jam I get in as easy as I did this one, Mr. Carter." He looked at Uncle Silas. "You sure gave me some good advice. I made an important discovery today."

Silas grinned at the young man. "If you'd listen to me more, you'd know more, Jeff," he teased. "But you're doing fine for a young fellow."

There was a comfortable silence between them for a few minutes until Silas asked suddenly, "You going back to the brigade tomorrow?"

"Yes, sir. I've got to get back. I've been gone too long."

"Well, I'll be praying for you and your father and brother. It may be a hard fight."

"I appreciate that. We need all the prayer we can get." When they got to the house, he got down and added, "I'll be praying for you too. My prayers don't amount to much, I guess. They're not very flowery like that preacher's this morning."

Silas stopped suddenly, turned, and fixed his eyes on the boy. "God's not looking for flowery prayer," he said evenly. "He's looking for hearts that are right and opened to His will. Remember that, Jeff."

"Yes, sir, I will."

"Don't know why we try to be so fancy with the Lord," Silas pondered. "He must get tired of our foolishness sometimes."

"I guess so, Mr. Carter."

"Well, you and Tom will have to come and see me when you get back to Richmond."

"We sure will—but I don't know when that will be."

Jeff turned down Silas's invitation to stay the night and instead reported to the officer-in-charge for his company. He said, "I'd like to catch up with my brigade as soon as possible."

The lieutenant replied, "That won't be hard. We're sending some reinforcements. You can go with them tomorrow morning. Your pa will be glad to see you." He hesitated, "Or maybe he won't. Be hard on a father seeing his son go beside him into the bloody fight we're likely to have."

Jeff spoke up at once. "I want to be with my father and brother—and with the Stonewall Brigade."

The lieutenant grinned. "I wish we had another twenty thousand like you," he said. "We need them against that passel of Yankees that's coming!"

5
The Army Pulls Out

Jeff quickly discovered that this departure of re-servists to replenish the brigade was little like the scenes he remembered from when he and his father had pulled out with the main brigade the previous year. As he joined the men gathered to form this replacement unit at dawn, he saw no bands and no crowds.

He thought back to when the Stonewall Brigade had marched out before the Battle of Bull Run. The air then had been filled with the sound of gunfire, bugles, and stirring songs. The streets were lined with cheering throngs, relatives and friends of the brave soldiers who looked so sharp in their soft gray uniforms and shining black leather boots. The excitement had stirred his own blood as he marched with his brigade.

By contrast, today's makeshift company looked more like a ragtag collection of ruffians bent on mischief. There were hardly any hardy young men in the group. Instead, most were either older, gray-haired patriots or boys scarcely older than Jeff. No one had a complete uniform, and fewer than half were armed. Old muzzle-loading muskets were standard; no one had a sleek breechloading rifle.

The sergeant in charge was distinguished by voice rather than uniform. His bellows bullied and pushed the raw recruits into line. "Fall in! Line up!

How do you pansies think you can fight the Yankees if you can't even line up to march?"

As far as Jeff could see, his bullying didn't help a great deal. Smiling at the sergeant's growing frustration, Jeff took his place in line and wished he had his drum so that he could add a little order to the sorry-looking group. *But,* he reflected, *they wouldn't know how to respond to the drum signals anyway.*

The men grew restless at the continuing delay as the sergeant rushed around making sure all their supplies were loaded and all the wagon drivers took their proper order. Jeff shifted from one foot to the other, wishing they were already finished with the long march.

Daydreaming about settling back into the routine of brigade life, he didn't hear at first as his name was shouted. Finally he realized the angry sergeant was yelling *his* name, and he turned quickly to respond.

To his surprise, he saw the Driscoll carriage pull up twenty yards short of the troop. Lucy disembarked like a princess, leaning on Old Sam's arm as she carefully stepped to the dusty ground and lifted her skirts just high enough to keep them clean but not high enough to provoke catcalls from the assembled men. The brilliant blue of her day dress was in stark contrast to the drab surroundings.

Lucy's gaze almost instantly rested on Jeff, and as it did she raised a dainty gloved hand to wave, and a clear, broad smile broke across her face.

She called, "Jeff! Jeff!" and he ducked his head in embarrassment.

The grizzled sergeant threw up his hands in mock disgust, grinning at this new, but not unwelcome, interruption to his attempts to call his men to order. His wide grin revealed the dark gaps of missing teeth, and his shout carried across the assembly area. "Which one of you fellers is Jeff?" he demanded.

Seeing no hope of escaping the ridicule of his jealous companions, Jeff promptly stepped out and lifted his arm in a half salute. "That's me, Sergeant."

The sergeant grinned more broadly. "Looks like you got somebody wants to see you off real proper, soldier. Go get your kiss and fall back in, quick like."

Jeff moved briskly toward Lucy and away from the hoots and hollers of the troop, whose comments followed him the whole way. "Give 'er a kiss for me, Jeff boy . . . If'n you don't want 'er, I'll take 'er. . . . Whoo! Whoo! Ain't she a purty one!"

Jeff's face was flaming by the time he reached Lucy's side. He grabbed her arm and muttered, "Let's get out of sight, Lucy. You shouldn't be hearing such things!"

Lucy giggled and clasped her hand over his as it still gripped her other arm. "I brought you some food for your long march, Jeff. You said how much you liked our Rosalee's fried chicken, and I couldn't stand to think of you on the road with nothing but hardtack. I've got a bundle all made up special for you in the carriage."

Jeff pulled her quickly around to the other side of the carriage, away from the eyes of the troops, and turned to her, his expression betraying his confused feelings of embarrassment, irritation, and pleasure. "I didn't expect to see you here."

"You should know, Jeff. I had to come and say good-bye to you!" She smiled shyly.

"Do your folks know you're here?"

Lucy shook her head. The golden curls swung around her shoulders, and she said lightly, "Oh, I'll tell them when I get back."

Jeff stared at her for a moment, then shook his head and grinned. "You sure lead your folks a merry chase. Don't you ever ask them for permission?"

"Only if I have to." She winked and laughed. Then she explained that she had risen early that morning and cajoled Sam into bringing her to the camp. She had hinted to Sam that her father had agreed to the trip, but she carefully explained to Jeff that she never actually said she had talked to him. Sam finally gave in, as he always did eventually.

"And so here I am, and here you are, and Daddy will just have to understand later!"

Jeff squeezed her arm. "Just so you don't go doing something really dangerous. I guess your father knows Sam'll take care of you."

"It's dangerous for you going off to war, Jeff," Lucy replied, tears welling up in her eyes. "I wish you weren't going. How long do you think it will take the army to whip the Yankees this time?" Despite her tearful entreaty, she also seemed a little bit excited to think about the Confederates routing the Union army.

Jeff stared at her. "I don't know. There's a big bunch of them, from what I hear, and we have a long way to go. It won't be a simple trouncing like you think. It might take a long time, and a lot of grief."

Lucy watched his face carefully. She frowned then and bit her lower lip. It made a rather fetching sight—and she was certainly aware of that fact.

She leaned toward him and whispered, "Be careful. I couldn't stand it if something happened to you."

"Oh, shucks, Lucy." Jeff shrugged. "I'll be all right. Don't worry about me."

"But I do worry about you," she said. "I want you to promise me that you won't take any chances."

At that Jeff smiled broadly. "Can't promise that—" he chuckled "—without promising to stay in bed the rest of my life. If a man's going to live, he's going to take chances. He just needs to pick the situations where it's worth taking a chance." Jeff paused, and his face turned serious. "When the minié balls start flying, they don't have any sense. Anybody could get shot."

Lucy looked troubled at Jeff's last remark. She had no relatives in the war—no brothers or sisters at all—and her uncles were working like her father to be sure the troops were supplied, so they weren't active soldiers either. Perhaps, for the first time, Lucy was beginning to feel some of the anxiety others had felt since the beginning. Her life had been caught up in parties and clothes, but now the reality of war was changing her.

"All right, get ready. Line up . . ." the sergeant began to call.

"I-I'll write you all the time, Jeff," she whispered.

Jeff felt embarrassed. "That'll be good. But I don't think the mail will keep up with us."

"Then I'll give you all the letters when you get back!"

"It's pretty hard to write on a march, Lucy . . . no paper or ink . . . and mostly we're too tired. Don't count on hearing much from me."

"Do you write to Leah, Jeff?"

Awkwardly Jeff shrugged. "I did, Lucy, but now —well, to tell the truth, we had a fight."

Lucy seemed surprised. "Do you two fight often?"

"Hardly ever, and I wish we hadn't this time."

"Well, people get into arguments. It happens to the best of us, but we don't have to like it!"

Lucy's words reminded Jeff of their own disagreement, recently mended. "You're right, Lucy. I made up with you, and I guess I need to with Leah too." He sighed. "I guess I will write—to both you and Leah. At least when I can." He laughed. "Seems like all I do these days is tell girls I'm sorry for acting like a fool!"

Lucy touched his arm lightly. "I'll look forward to your letters, Jeff. I'll be praying for you. Take care!"

"You too, Lucy," Jeff responded. "Well, I'd better get back to my company."

They walked together around the carriage, and Lucy beckoned to Sam, who quickly swung down a large bundle wrapped in brown paper.

Jeff took it gratefully, saying, "Thanks a lot, Lucy."

There were almost back to the waiting soldiers when Lucy suddenly reached up, turned him toward her, and—before Jeff knew what was happening—stood on tiptoe and planted a loud kiss on his cheek. "There!" she exclaimed. "You come back safe, you hear?" She turned and ran back to the carriage.

Jeff endured the stares and teasing of his comrades as he took his place in the ranks. The sergeant, moving along the line, said with a grin,

"Reckon that kiss'll have to do you until we get those blue-bellies whupped!" Then he hollered, "All right, forward, march!"

As Jeff moved out with his company, he glanced over his shoulder and saw the Driscolls' carriage disappearing in the opposite direction. He couldn't help feeling a little proud that Lucy had thought enough of him to rise early and come bid him good-bye.

In the small town of Chantilly, Virginia, the Army of Northern Virginia waited. The Southerners had fought hard against Pope at Second Manassas and now were resting, recouping the strength, arms, ammunition, and soldiers they had lost in battle.

When Jeff and his makeshift company arrived at the camp, Jeff questioned his sergeant. "Reckon I can find the Stonewall Brigade around here, Sarge?"

The sergeant grinned, his gapped-tooth smile mocking. "Seems to me if'n I was you, I'd be lookin' for that purty gal, 'stead of a pack of ugly Stonewall soldiers, boy." He laughed and then directed Jeff toward the Stonewall encampment. His voice followed him: "Guess some other fellers'll be romancing your woman while you're helping Stonewall. Get on with you, now!"

Jeff managed to grin, waved at his fellow soldiers, and made his way through the camp. A few questions led him to a spot on the outside of the main army camp where he began to see his old companions.

Soon he spotted Sergeant Henry Mapes.

"Sergeant! Sergeant Mapes!"

Mapes, a tall, rangy man of thirty-five with black hair and eyes, turned and waited until Jeff came running up to him. He stuck out his hand and grasped Jeff's. "Well, Private Majors, you finally decided to join the army?"

"I just got back, Sergeant," Jeff replied. He looked around and asked, "Where's the rest of the company?"

"This way, son," Mapes motioned with a long arm. "I'll take you right to them. Your pa will be right glad to see you, and Tom too."

As they walked along, Jeff asked, "Was it bad —that last fight at Manassas?"

Mapes shook his head. "We whupped them, but we got shot up pretty good. We lost Lieutenant Mayfer. He got shot right off—right in the heart."

"Oh, no! Not Lieutenant Mayfer! I hate it! He was a good officer."

"Sure was," Sergeant Mapes agreed. "Besides that, we lost Haynes, Tolliver, Coleman, and that young one that just joined, Henry Simms."

As they approached the Stonewall encampment, Jeff was silent, his sense of loss weighing his shoulders down, causing his face to reflect the sorrow he felt. He had known these men well, all of them. Young Simms had been a particularly close friend. He finally asked, "It *was* bad, wasn't it, Sergeant?"

"It wasn't good," Mapes agreed. He was usually a cheerful man, but the grief on his face told Jeff more about the true nature of the battle than his brief comment. "We miss them—every one of them. And not just because we need the manpower. We'll likely get replacements soon, but you can't replace a friend that easy."

"I came with the replacement troops," Jeff offered. Then he saw his father walking up ahead with another officer. He wanted to run to him and be grabbed in his big bear hug, but that wouldn't have been military. He walked slowly beside Sergeant Mapes until his father turned and saw him.

Jeff had his father's dark hair and tan skin. Captain Nelson Major's hazel eyes fell on Jeff, and at once he broke out, "Jeff!" and came running, his arms outstretched. When he had almost reached Jeff, he seemed to realize that the other men were watching him with amusement. He abruptly stopped, nodded toward his son, and called out, "Private Majors. You're back, I see." Then he couldn't contain himself but reached out and gave Jeff his bear hug anyway, squashing Jeff's arm between them and catching him in the midst of a proper military salute in respect of his father's rank. "It's good to see you, son. I've been worried about you."

Jeff had the breath almost squeezed out of him by his father's powerful arms. He stammered, embarrassed, "I'm the one that's been worried, Pa— Captain. Sergeant Mapes been telling me what a hard fight it was."

Captain Majors regained his composure and stepped back, adjusting his uniform jacket. "Yes, it was, and a harder one's coming up, I'm afraid. Son, how's my baby Esther?"

Jeff could see his father's eyes glisten as he asked about the baby daughter he hardly knew. "She's growing just great! The Carters love her like their own, and she's got Ma's sunny disposition!" Jeff looked at his father, hoping to ease some of his sadness.

His father merely nodded, then said, "Go find Tom. He's worried about you too. We'll have time later for you to tell what happened in Kentucky."

"Yes, sir!"

Jeff greeted other friends as he moved through the camp, and he quickly found his brother. Tom was now a sergeant, and the two had a glad moment of reunion.

It had been a long, hard march for Jeff, and as the air grew cooler and the sun began to set, he realized how ravenously hungry he was and how exhausted he felt.

"Come on, let's see if we can find some grub," Tom said as he grabbed his hat and mess kit. He led Jeff to the company cook tent, where Jeff was welcomed by more friends.

He was shocked, however, at the appearance of the men. They were gaunt and unshaven; their shaggy hair poked through the holes in their shapeless hats. The uniforms on many of them hung in tatters, some of them held their pants up with lengths of rope. Their bodies were as grimy and mud-caked as their uniforms. Many didn't wear shoes or boots. Only their guns were clean and shining.

Later Jeff whispered to Tom, "I had no idea everything and everybody was so run down and run out. Why, I feel terrible with my fine new clothes and boots while some of our friends don't even have anything on their feet!"

Tom looked around sadly and then put a comforting hand on Jeff's shoulder. "The supplies you all brought will at least get everyone into shoes of one kind or another, and the soap'll help us clean up some—but it's the truth, we're pretty worn down.

We're not fit to go into battle, but I reckon we're gonna do what we gotta do."

They were sitting in front of a campfire, eating cornbread, some salt pork (carefully divided out among the troops), and the last of Lucy's food packet. There wasn't much left after Jeff had shared it on the road with the replacement troops and then handed out most of the rest to his friends who seemed the hungriest.

Sitting with them around the fire were the men of his father's squad, the men he knew best. Charlie Bowers, at fourteen, was the youngest of the troop, small, and, as Jeff's father liked to say, "not yet growed into his feet." His tow head and bright blue eyes made him stand out in any company.

Jeff handed Charlie the last of Lucy's cake, and he gobbled it down as fast as he could. His eyes were on the piece Jeff had given to Curly Henson, who laughed his thanks, saying, "You're welcome back, Jeff, but not so much as this cake!"

Curly Henson was a huge man with flaming red hair. He'd saved Jeff's life at Bull Run, and Jeff never really thought he would, since Curly had made life miserable for him. Since his rescue, Jeff and Curly had become fast friends.

Jed Hawkins, sitting just outside the main campfire light, began to strum on his guitar. He was a small, lean man with dark hair and black eyes that would glow as he sang one of the hundreds of songs he knew. He began to pluck out a tune, and Jeff smiled as he heard the words. Several of the men around began to sing along; others simply hummed or leaned back and listened.

"Let us close our game of poker,
   Take our tin cups in hand
   While we gather round the cook's tent door
   Where dry mummies of hard crackers
   Are given to each man;
   Oh, hard crackers, come again no more!

"There's a hungry, thirsty soldier,
   Who wears his life away,
   With torn clothes, whose better days are o'er;
   He is sighing now for lemonade,
   And with throat as dry as hay,
   Sings, 'Hard crackers, come again no more.'

" 'Tis the song that is uttered
   In camp by night and day,
   'Tis the wail that is mingled with each snore;
   'Tis the sighing of the soul
   For spring chickens far away,
   Oh, hard crackers, come again no more!"

"You can't sing any better than when I left,"
Jeff teased Jed. "And when are you going to learn
how to play that thing?"

Hawkins picked up a stick and threw it at Jeff,
who easily dodged. "I'll sing for them Yankees when
we meet up with them. They're going to appreciate
it. And if I'm as bad as you say, Jeff, maybe they'll
surrender just to get me to stop!"

The talk wandered around the campfire, most
of it concerning home, girls left behind, and the
prospects for the coming battle. Jeff finally asked,
"Where and when are we going? Does anybody
know?"

Curly Henson grinned at him. "Well, I was talking to Stonewall today. Me and him get together to
plan these battles, don't you see? What we agreed

on, with Marse Robert's permission, was to head on up into Maryland and whup the Yankees up there."

Laughter ran around the campfire.

Tom picked up a stick and began poking the fire, throwing sparks high into the air. "Well," he began, "I don't know as Curly arranged it or not, but the word I hear is that we're headed North."

The men had always respected what they heard from Tom. They knew he spent time in conversation with his father, who was one of Stonewall's planners.

Tom continued, "General Lee thinks he's got to attack. Got to take the war to the Yankees." He looked around at the others, noting, "In the first place, we've run out of just about everything. Get us up into Maryland, and we can get in on some of their August harvest while we leave our folks down here to get in our own harvest without us eating them out of everything. Besides that," he added, "if we can hit them hard enough, the English might come in on our side."

The talk continued sporadically, and then finally Tom ordered, "You fellers get on to bed. I got a feeling Stonewall's going to march our legs off, and it could be tomorrow."

After the others had crawled into their blankets, Jeff reached into his pocket. "Got a letter for you, Tom. It's from Sarah."

Tom took the letter and simply held it for a moment. He looked over at Jeff, his dark eyes reflecting the light of the fire. "She talk about me, Jeff?"

"She sure did. She misses you real bad, Tom." Jeff then told him about how Sarah had unceremoniously dumped young Matthew Henderson. "She sure put the skids on him, Tom. You just read that letter and see if she don't tell you all about it."

Tom opened the letter and moved closer to the dying fire. He read it slowly, then read it again.

Jeff turned his gaze away and sat staring into the fire. The air was filled with the sounds of a military camp: horses shifted and snorted on the lines, soldiers coughed and sometimes moaned in their sleep, the cooks banged the cooking pots as they finished late night cleanup and prepared the cold rations that had to be ready before dawn if the troops were to leave in the early morning. Somebody sang a sad song about how he was going to be killed in tomorrow's battle.

Finally, Tom folded Sarah's letter and put it in his inside pocket, close to his heart, saying to Jeff, "Well, I guess I won't get to see Sarah any time soon."

"Maybe sooner than you think," Jeff said quickly. "Maybe they'll send the army into Kentucky, and then we can stop by for a visit."

Tom laughed. "That'd be something. To bring the Army of Northern Virginia along when I go courting!" He slapped Jeff on the shoulder. "I'm glad you're back, brother," he said warmly. "I've missed you. Us Majorses got to stick together."

Jeff grinned. "It'll all be all right, you just wait and see."

The two of them rolled into their blankets.

Jeff knew there were only a few hours before reveille would waken them while it was still dark. He lay awake for a long time, however. He thought of Leah, of Lucy, of Esther, and of what it would be like in a world without war.

And then he thought about tomorrow.

6

The Lost Orders

Dan Carter endured the hardship of travel better than Leah and Ezra expected. The first week of September had brought cooling breezes, and though the sun was bright overhead during the day, the nights were pleasant enough. The three of them followed the track of the Army of the Potomac, which was moving to intercept the Army of Northern Virginia, headed by General Robert E. Lee.

One night Leah insisted that a party be held for all of the young men who had enlisted out of Pineville, Kentucky, the Carters' hometown. There was little argument about this, and, after darkness fell, Leah and Ezra welcomed the young men to a fine supper.

Jay Walters arrived first, with Leah's brother, Royal, both of them from Company A. Jay was nineteen, his straw-colored hair, brown eyes, and long, thin arms and legs earning him his nickname, Scarecrow.

Royal was only a year older. He was not tall but was thick and strong, with blond hair and blue eyes. He was called "the Professor" by the rest of the company because he had completed one year of college and was considered a budding scholar.

The two were soon joined by Dave Mellon, a red-haired, freckle-faced young man, son of the Pineville banker; and Walter Beddows, his close companion. Beddows was short, well-built, and had a shock of brown hair that continually fell into his eyes.

"All of you sit down," Leah said. "We've got a good meal for you."

She handed out plates heaped with beef, freshly baked bread, and the eternal army beans.

Then another soldier came. "Can anybody get in on this here party?"

"Ira!" Leah said. "I might have known you wouldn't miss a meal. Sit down, and I'll get you a plate."

She loaded a plate with a mountain of food and handed it to Ira Pickens. He was a tall boy, very homely, with bushy black hair. He had been a friend of Leah's since the first battle of the war. He had informed her then that he was raising her to be his girl friend when she got old enough. At seventeen, he was only two years older than Leah herself.

"Well, now, this is fine," Dan Carter said. "I sure do enjoy listening to you fellows eat." A laugh went up around the fire, and Dan looked fondly at the young men. "If you fellows can fight as well as you can eat, we won't have any trouble."

"Ah, we won't have any trouble anyway, Mr. Carter." Ira grinned. "This time we'll whip the Rebels and have this foolishness over with once and for all."

Royal chewed thoughtfully on a piece of beef. He shook his head slowly, saying, "We said that before, didn't we, Ira—at Bull Run? And at Seven Days, then at Second Manassas. You see, no matter how many men we take, the Rebels seem to send us back whupped to a frazzle."

"You know, that's right," Dave Mellon said. "I don't understand it. We've got better guns, better equipment, and there's more of us, but we never win. Why is that, do you think?"

Walter Beddows was a thoughtful young man. "Well, they're fighting for their homes, Dave. That's a little different. Imagine how hard you would fight if the Confederates came into Pineville, tearing up our place like we've done theirs."

"Well, they started it," Jay complained. "They can't fuss if we bring the war down to them."

"Let's not argue politics," Leah said. She was wearing her only dress that wasn't a work dress, a light green one that matched her eyes. Her blonde hair was fixed in a long braid that wrapped around her head like a crown, and she added a touch of femininity to the rough group of men.

The talk went on about the war, and she came and sat down close to her father, listening.

Finally Royal said, "We've got enough men this time, but nobody knows what Robert E. Lee will do. That man is sure hard to handle."

"A fine Christian man from all I've heard," Dan Carter said. "As is Stonewall Jackson."

"I don't see how Christians can fight Christians," Walter complained.

"That's just the way it is." Royal sighed. "We think we're doing God's will, and they think they're doing God's will."

"Well, we both can't be right," Jay put in.

"Why, of course we can't," Ira said. He was an outspoken young man, long and lanky. He stuffed an enormous chunk of cake into his mouth and swallowed, seemingly without chewing.

Leah giggled, and he looked over at her and smiled. "Don't you laugh at the way I eat my vittles, Leah!"

Then he began to explain how the Federal Army couldn't fail this time. "This time we'll be fighting on our own ground."

"How's that, Ira?" Jay asked.

"Shoot, ain't you figured it out yet, Jay?"

"No, I ain't." Jay winked at Leah. He liked to pull Ira's leg, so he innocently asked, "How have you and the generals got it planned?"

Ira licked his fingers, then shrugged. "Stands to reason we been losing because we been in their front yard—the Rebels' front yard, that is. All the battles been in the South."

"Well, that's where the war is," Jay argued. "We got to go there and fight 'em."

"That's right," Leah agreed. "That's what the war is about—whether they got the right to leave the Union or not."

"Sure it is," Jay said. "They *want* to leave the Union, and Abe don't want 'em to do it."

"So we got to go South and whup 'em until they agree to stay in," Ira answered. "But the way I see it, we been losing battles because this is their land. They'll fight hard to keep it, and they know their way around, and we don't."

"I think that's right, Ira," Mr. Carter remarked. He had obviously thought about this. "Sometimes our men just plain get lost, but the Confederates— why, it's their home."

"That's just what I said." Ira grinned. "But if what we hear about the Rebs coming up North is true, that'll be a different story." He leaned back, saying grandly, "Oh, we'll have 'em this time, no doubt about it!"

His confidence amused the others, but Ira refused to back down. "You just wait," he promised. "We'll get Bobby Lee this time!"

Later, after the others had gone, Leah asked, "What's wrong, Ezra? You haven't said ten words."

"Oh, nothing," Ezra said quickly. "Just don't know much about battles, I guess."

"But you've been in battles."

"Just the first one—and I didn't see much of that."

Leah took a stick and doodled with it in the dirt. The fire sputtered, sending sparks dancing. Looking up, she made a statement, "You don't think we'll win this battle."

Ezra didn't answer at once. His face was highlighted by the flickering firelight, and he looked very young. "You know, Leah," he said finally, "in one way, nobody wins a battle."

"Why, Ezra, what does *that* mean?"

"Just that no matter which side *wins*, there's going to be lots of men dead and shot up—on both sides. If a mother hears her son's been killed, she won't care much who won the battle."

Leah nodded slowly. "You're right, Ezra. I've thought about that a lot too. Specially with Jeff and his folks on one side and my brother on this one."

Glancing at her, Ezra asked, "You worried about Jeff?"

"Yes—and about Royal and Ira—and all of them."

They sat silently, looking into the fire, and at

last Leah said, "I guess there's nothing left to say. Words don't change war. I'm going to bed."

"I'm praying for Jeff," Ezra said quietly.

Leah looked at him, startled. "That's good of you, Ezra. He wasn't very nice to you when he left."

"Aw, he didn't mean nothing, Leah. And he didn't mean to leave mad at you either," Ezra said, getting to his feet. "Good night. I'll see you in the morning."

When he had gone, Leah climbed inside the wagon to her cubbyhole, created by hanging a blanket across half of the wagon's interior. She carefully removed her day dress, folded it, smoothed out the wrinkles, and laid it in her traveling trunk. She pulled a faded but clean work dress from a nearby hook and slipped it over her shoulders. She'd learned last trip out with her father that a young lady must always keep her modesty—even in her own wagon at night—when traveling with an army of young men.

She dropped gratefully to her narrow cot and pulled the quilt over her. From underneath the wagon she heard her father's uneven breathing. She knew he wasn't feeling well. *Lord, let Pa get well,* she prayed silently, *and take care of all the boys.*

Neither Leah and the Yanks nor Jeff and the Rebs could have anticipated what would happen at the Battle of Antietam, but it nearly changed the course of the war. Folks on both sides later called it the Case of the Lost Orders. Much later, Leah's brother explained it to her.

On September 9, General Lee issued Special Order Number One Ninety-one. In it he set forth the complete battle plans for the Confederate Army. This involved splitting his rather small army into four different parts. This was very dangerous in the face of the Union force of 90,000 men, but Lee was confident. He knew that General McClellan was a timid leader and not likely to attack. He was aware also that McClellan had received wrong information about the size of the Southern army. McClellan always thought he was vastly outnumbered, when in fact he himself always had a larger force.

The four Confederate columns went their separate directions, but at noon on September 13 a copy of Special Order Number One Ninety-one fell into McClellan's hands. It was addressed to Confederate Major General D. H. Hill and had been found wrapped around three cigars at an abandoned campsite. No one ever discovered who was responsible for such strange treatment of an important document.

When McClellan read the plans, he had one of his men identify the handwriting as that of Robert E. Lee. Then he held the document high, crying out, "If I can't whip Bobby Lee with this, I'll turn in my stars and go home."

And so it was that when the two armies came together at a small town called Sharpsburg and a creek called Antietam, General George McClellan had the complete battle plan of the Confederate Army in his hands. He also had an enormous army.

But neither the Carters nor the Majorses knew all this before the battle. They only knew that, no matter the outcome of the battle, many men would lose their lives, and their families would mourn their losses.

By the time the Union army pulled up in front of Antietam Creek, Dan Carter had become very ill indeed. He could barely get out of Leah's small cot, and Ezra said under his breath, "Leah, I don't like the way your pa looks. Maybe we'd better turn around and go home."

Leah bit her lip nervously but shook her head. "You don't know my pa," she said. "When he sets out to do something, he'll do it."

"Well, maybe we can get one of the army doctors to come take a look at him."

Leah nodded at once. "That's a good idea, Ezra. I'll go ask Major Bates to send one of the surgeons by."

Major Silas Bates, commander of the Washington Blues, was a tall man with a powerful voice. He had become very friendly with the Carters; he said he appreciated all they did for his men.

He agreed at once. "Why, of course. I'll have Dr. Johnson come by and take a look at him."

Dr. Johnson examined Dan Carter carefully and afterwards spoke quietly and seriously with him. "You're a sick man, Mr. Carter. You don't have any business here in this sort of thing."

Dan Carter smiled and buttoned up his shirt. His voice was weak, but there was purpose in his eyes. "Yes, I do have business being here, Dr. Johnson. God has told me to come and minister to these soldier boys, and I'm going to do it."

Johnson stared at him and then shook his head. He walked away, motioning to Leah to follow. When they were out of hearing, he advised, "Keep your father in bed as much as you can. I won't be able to come back, because once the battle starts, I'll have all I can do."

Leah thanked the doctor and went back to sit beside her father, saying sternly, "Now, I'm going to boss you, Pa. You've told me what to do all my life, and now the tables have turned. You're going to stay in that bed, and I'm going to take care of you like you're baby Esther."

He smiled and patted her hand. "Well, I guess you've got the best of the argument, daughter. I don't feel too good, to tell the truth."

All afternoon Ezra and Leah kept a close watch on the sick man. After Ezra chopped enough wood for the night's cooking fire, he went to relieve Leah at her father's bedside. He remarked, "I guess it's a good thing I'm a Christian now, because I can pray for your pa to get well, can't I?"

"Yes, you can. And God truly hears us. We both will," Leah answered quickly. And she added to herself, *I'll pray for every soldier tonight, blue or gray.*

Later that night, the army bedded down, and Royal found his way to the Carters' supper wagon. He visited with his father for a while, then came to sit with Ezra and Leah in front of the glowing fire.

Everywhere Leah looked out into the darkness, what seemed to be thousands of fires winked and sputtered. After they sat quietly for a time, she whispered, "Royal, I'm afraid. It's going to be a big battle, isn't it?"

"It looks like it. I believe the Rebels brought every man they could with them. They're over there across the creek, and there is no way to get them except to go after them."

Quietness reigned around the fire, and then Ezra said, "I wish I could go with you fellers, but I gave my promise that I wouldn't to Mr. Silas. It didn't seem fair for him to help me escape so I could fight against the Confederates again."

"You take care of Leah and Pa," Royal said. "That's all I ask."

Then Royal got up, and Leah went over and hugged him. "You be careful, you hear? Don't try to be a hero."

"Why, we're all heroes in the Washington Blues," Royal said, trying to smile at her. His solemn voice betrayed him as he added, "If anything should happen to me, don't forget I'll be with the Lord."

As soon as he was gone, Leah sat down heavily, blinking back her tears. "I hate this war," she said through clenched teeth.

"I guess everybody does," Ezra answered. He sat for a long time, seemingly not knowing what to say. "I guess you're worried about Jeff and his family too. I know I am."

Leah thought about how she and Jeff had parted, angry words still hanging between them. She turned to Ezra. "I was so mean to him, Ezra. When he left, I wouldn't even give him a kind word."

"Well, you can do that the next time you see him."

But Leah's face creased deeper in sadness. "I wish he knew how sorry I am about the way I fought with him."

"You can write him a letter after the battle."

But Leah was troubled. "But what if he gets—" She broke off, and her lips trembled. She didn't even want to say the words *if he gets killed*. She looked up at Ezra and whispered, "Why did I do it, Ezra?"

"Argue with Jeff?" Ezra shrugged his shoulders. "Why, shoot, Leah, we all do stuff like that. And men are faster to argue with and harder to get along with anyhow. You should know that from your pa and your brother."

"Pa's the least fightingest man I know! He doesn't hardly ever get angry."

"No, I reckon he don't. But he's been a Christian a long time."

"I don't think I'll ever grow up!" Leah lowered her eyes, then looked up with tears. "I'm so selfish, Ezra!"

Ezra shifted his feet and wouldn't raise his eyes to meet hers. He was obviously uncomfortable. "Well, I don't know, Leah, about how to stop being selfish. In the first place, you ain't all that bad."

"Yes, I am! Why, I am quite likely the most selfish girl in all of Kentucky!"

Ezra smiled, looking at her, her hands on her hips, her lower lip thrust out. "Just as well you think so, I guess. No better incentive to make a change! But whether you know it or not, Leah Carter, you're a sweet, loving girl—that's what you are!"

Leah was startled by Ezra's words. Her cheeks flushed, and now it was her turn to stare at the ground, not meeting his eyes. She protested, "You don't know me very well if you think that."

"Sure I do! I know you better than I've ever known any girl. You're worrying yourself to death over being mean—but if you were as selfish as you claim, you wouldn't have rescued me."

"I wouldn't?"

"Nope. Mean folks seem to just enjoy being mean."

Leah fixed her large eyes on the tall boy for a long moment. "You sure do know how to make me feel better, Ezra," she said finally. "Even if I'm not sure I believe you." She smiled and added, "I'm glad you're here with us. I feel lots safer with you around, especially with my father like he is now."

"I'm glad of that," Ezra said. "Now, what we have to do is get your pa all well, get Royal and Ira and the others through the battle safe, and pray that Jeff and his folks make it."

"That's a lot, isn't it, Ezra?"

"Well—as your pa would say—for us, maybe, but not for God!"

7

Stonewall Takes a Ferry

As the Army of Northern Virginia prepared for battle, more than a few agreed that they had suffered ill fortune since leaving Virginia. General Lee had been thrown by his horse, Traveler, badly injuring both wrists. He could not ride now but had to be driven in a wagon. Strangely enough, Stonewall Jackson had also been thrown by his horse, and the fall had badly wrenched his back, so that he had trouble making the journey. The leader of the second corps, General James Longstreet, had blisters on his feet so bad that he couldn't walk and had to ride wherever he went.

It was a ragtag army indeed that made its way through Maryland. Many of the men had no shoes at all. And worse than the pain of cut feet was their gnawing hunger.

Long after, Leah would read a newspaper account of one Confederate's experience. Private Alexander Hunter of the Seventeenth Virginia wrote home, "For six days, not a morsel of meat or bread had gone into our stomachs. Our menu consisted of apples and corn."

But the Southern army toiled on, ill and exhausted. Some fell too far behind to catch up. Some simply refused to go, insisting they had enlisted to defend their homeland, not to invade the North. In all, about fifteen hundred men dropped out of Lee's army during the march.

As the troops approached a high bluff, Jeff rattled out the orders on his drum, then his company drew up on the edge of the cliff. Far below, as in the bottom of a bowl, lay Harper's Ferry.

Jeff's father studied the town and said, "I'd rather take that place forty times than try to defend it once."

Jeff nodded. "And so it's good we're on the side that's doing the taking, Pa—Captain. We sorely need the ammunition and supplies we'll find down below."

The battle was relatively simple. Stonewall Jackson had brought three divisions to do the job, and there was never any question about the Confederates' superiority, even in their bedraggled state. The armory was impossible to defend, and soon Jackson and his men had performed one of the great feats of the war: they captured the armory plus 11,000 Union troops, not to mention an enormous amount of supplies, including badly needed muskets and cannons.

Despite this victory, the Confederates had little time to savor it or to rest. Orders came for the Stonewall Brigade and the rest of Jackson's troops to come at once to Sharpsburg.

The troops arrived so tired they could hardly stand up. The officers led them to their positions along the creek.

"We'll be the Confederate left," Tom told Jeff and the rest of the squad. "I expect they'll be coming right across that cornfield, so try to sleep while you can."

Stars overhead spangled the velvet blackness of the night. Jeff lay looking up. He knew that Charlie Bowers, who lay next to him, was badly scared, so he tried to reassure him, urging, "Don't worry, Charlie. God will look out for us."

But even Jeff, with aching bones and sore feet, dreaded to see morning come. He'd heard rumors that there were 100,000 Yankees across Antietam Creek, and he fully expected half that number to come charging through the cornfield right at the Stonewall Brigade.

Charlie turned to look at him, his youthful face tense. "Aren't you scared, Jeff?"

"About the battle tomorrow?"

"What else? Of course. Are you afraid?"

"I guess I have to admit it—at least a little."

"Me too."

Jeff rolled over and saw that his friend was as tense as a wire spring. "You know, Charlie, I guess if we went down this line and asked every soldier, 'Are you scared?' most of them would say they are."

Charlie considered this, then objected, "Some of them don't act scared."

"I hope I don't show it. But most of us spend a lot of time putting on an act—and a lot of time praying."

This seemed to interest Charlie. He propped himself up on his elbow and peered at Jeff. "How's that?"

"Oh, I reckon you know." Jeff shrugged. "Lots of stuff goes on inside of us that we wouldn't like everybody to know about."

"What kind of stuff?" Charlie pursued.

Jeff squirmed, then said, "Look, have you ever had a fight with someone just before church?"

"Sure!"

"Well, when you went to the service, what'd you do?"

"Nothing much."

"Yes, you did." Jeff grinned at him. "You didn't go around scowling and hitting people. You stood up and sang the hymns and bowed your head when the preacher prayed. You acted nice, even if you were boiling over inside."

Charlie was somewhat shocked. "How'd you know I done like that, Jeff?"

"Because I've done the same thing. And so have most of the fellows in this line. I guess we don't think much about it at the time, but we hide a lot of what goes on inside us."

"Be pretty awful if we didn't, wouldn't it?"

Jeff lay back and looked up at the stars that glittered overhead. He could hear the sound of men moving restlessly, and from far away came the mournful sound of a dog howling. "I guess so—but it's not exactly honest to put on an act."

Charlie lay back too, and Jeff listened to the sounds of the night.

Finally Charlie murmured, "Well, I'll pray for you, and you pray for me. All right, Jeff?"

"Sure, Charlie, that's fine! We all better be praying up a storm, come dawn!"

8
The Eve of Battle

Leah returned to the wagon and found her father sleeping fitfully on the cot she had made up for him. After watching him for a few minutes, her heart heavy, she heard Ezra's distinctive whistle and looked up to see him coming from the small creek that ran behind their camp.

Ezra had been washing clothes. He nodded to her and began to hang the wet clothes on the ropes he'd hung between two saplings. "He's been kind of restless, Leah. He's had a fever too, I think."

Leah watched him hang up her father's favorite linsey-woolsey white shirt and add to it several garments of his own. "You didn't have to do that," she said. "I'll do the washing."

"Aw, it weren't no trouble." Ezra shrugged. "I never did mind washing."

"You're different from most men." She smiled. "I think Jeff would wear a shirt till it turned stiff as a board with sweat and dirt before he would wash it."

The mention of Jeff brought a quick frown to her face, and she covered it hurriedly by saying, "They're talking all up and down the line about the battle that's coming. Everybody thinks it's going to be a bad one."

"I don't think there are any good ones, are there?"

"No, not really. But you know what I mean, Ezra." She moved over to where the food was stored in a sturdy pine box, lifted the top, and began to take out yeast starter, flour, lard, salt, and a pinch of her precious sugar. "I think I'll make some biscuits. Will you set up my Dutch oven?"

Ezra had finished hanging up the clothes. "Sure I will," he said. "Nothing like hot biscuits. I wish we had some sorghum from that mill Mr. Silas had down in Richmond. That was good, wasn't it?"

Leah nodded. "I worry about Uncle Silas sometimes, but the last letter we got said he was doing fine."

Soon the smell of stew cooking was in the air. Biscuits were browning in the Dutch oven, and the sky was beginning to darken. Leah added a scant measure of fresh ground coffee to the morning's grounds, poured in fresh spring water, and set the pot to boil by the side of the cooking fire.

From far away a soldier with a fine tenor voice began singing. She sat listening, and Ezra, who had been adding wood to the fire, stopped to listen also as the plaintive words hovered over the sprawling camp.

> "Just before the battle, Mother,
> I am thinking most of you,
> While upon the field we're watching
> With the enemy in view.
> Comrades brave are round me lying,
> Filled with thoughts of home and God;
> For well they know that on the morrow
> Some will sleep beneath the sod."

As the young soldier's voice faltered, other voices joined in on the chorus:

> "Farewell, Mother, you may never
> Press me to your heart again;
> But O, you'll not forget me, Mother,
> If I'm numbered with the slain."

The night was quiet, and the voices clear as bells. The words carried over the fields, and no one could tell where the Union voices ended and the Confederate voices began.

> "Oh, I long to see you, Mother,
> And the loving ones at home,
> But I'll never leave our banner
> Till in honor I can come.
> Tell the traitors all around you
> That their cruel words, we know,
> In every battle kill our soldiers
> By the help they give the foe."

When the last notes died away, Leah gave a slight shudder. "I don't like that song," she said. "It's too sad. I wish he hadn't started it."

Ezra looked down to his right along the line and nodded. "General Mac over there, I guess he's doing some heavy thinking. He can't afford to let the Rebs whup us this time."

General McClellan stood before his officers and examined them carefully. All day he'd been getting little information, and now as dark blanketed the field he said irritably, "I have no idea where Jackson is."

General Hooker, standing across the table, asserted, "He's right across that creek, General. I'd bet my right eye on it."

Hooker was a big, fine-looking soldier called "Fighting Joe Hooker." He had little respect for McClellan as a fighting general, believing that he himself would do a better job.

McClellan moved nervously. He was a small, dapper man, who wore his uniform proudly. He had been president of a railroad before the war, and his soldiers adored him. They called him "Little Mac," and no matter how many times he lost, they never lost faith in him.

McClellan looked down at the map in front of him and ran his finger along a twisting, winding line. "Antietam Creek," he said. "All we have to do is get across, and we'll have them."

"Might be harder than you think, General," another officer said. "The Rebs have had plenty of time to get in place over there."

McClellan nodded. "They're a big force." He turned to Hooker. "I want you to lead the attack against the Confederate left in the morning."

"Yes, General. You can count on me. My boys are ready for a fight."

McClellan turned to look out the door of the tent. There was a nervousness in his mannerisms that the officers didn't like. He showed none of the confidence that he usually manifested.

After the officers had left the tent, Hooker said to his second in command, "McClellan's good at training troops, but he's worthless as a fighting general."

While the Union generals talked, across the creek the Confederates were digging in. Tom Majors grabbed a shovel and was helping the members of the squad. He made the dirt fly for a while, then looked up and said, "I reckon they'll be coming at us with everything they've got, Curly."

Curly Henson, sweat running down his face, stopped working on the long defensive trench and nodded. "I wish that creek was as big as the Mississippi River!" he muttered. "And I wish all them Yankees were right in the pit."

Jed Hawkins, who had stripped off his shirt to do his part of the work, laughed. "Don't wish that. Stonewall would send us right into the pit after them! There ain't nothing that man won't do!"

All up and down the line, members of the Stonewall Brigade were throwing up whatever protection they could. They knew that there would be no time to put up a defense in the morning.

"Where's Jeff?" Tom asked suddenly. "I haven't seen him nearly all day."

Charlie Bowers was too small to do much work. He was helping Sergeant Henry Mapes drag some brush to put in front of a hole. "Jeff's pretty bad sick, Tom," he said. "I think he's lying down back in the shade."

Tom straightened suddenly. "He hasn't felt good since he got back. I'll go check on him."

Leaving his team digging ditches and dragging fence posts into position, Tom made his way to the big firs that lifted their heads farther back from the creek. He found his father squatting beside Jeff, who was sitting with his back to one of the huge trees.

Tom saw at once that Jeff's face was pale and knew that he was very ill. "What's the matter, Jeff?" he asked. "Got a stomachache?"

Jeff's opened his eyes with an effort. "I wish it

was just a stomachache," he whispered. "That's what I thought it was myself at first."

Tom looked at his father and saw that he was worried. "A lot of us got stomachaches from all those green apples we've been eating."

"It's more than that, Tom," Captain Majors said, then spoke to Jeff. "I wish I could send you back, son. You don't need to be anywhere near this fight."

Jeff shook his head, his lips a thin white line. "Don't worry about me, Captain. I'll be all right."

Captain Majors hesitated and then said, "Tom, you stay here with him. I've got to go have a meeting with the staff officers."

"Yes, sir."

Nelson Majors hurried to General Lee's headquarters. It was no more than a tent hastily thrown up, but a large group of officers was gathered.

General Lee moved about carefully, holding his hands away from his body. They were still sore from the fall he'd taken. To his left, Stonewall Jackson, with his cap pulled down over his eyes, watched every move Lee made; and to the right, the big, burly Longstreet did the same.

Lee had been speaking, but his eyes caught Majors as he came hurrying up. "Ah, glad to have you with us, Captain. We'll be needing all the engineers we can get. We need to throw up more reinforcements if possible."

Stonewall said, "General, why don't we just charge across that creek? They won't be expecting us. We can catch them off guard."

Lee smiled faintly. It was so much like Stonewall Jackson. They were here against a force twice as big as their own, and he wanted to charge!

"I hardly think that's the answer, General Jackson. We'll take the defensive ground this time. Perhaps we'll be able to mount a charge later on." He stepped forward and with the toe of his boot drew a crooked line. "This is the creek, gentlemen. We'll mount our defense like this. General Jackson, you will take the left. General Hill, you'll take the center, and General Longstreet the right." He marked each spot on the ground with his toe and stood staring at it.

"Who do you think will be coming at us, sir?" Longstreet asked.

"Our scouts inform me that Hooker will be coming to our left. That will be for you, General Jackson. General Sumner will be coming at the middle, and Burnside will be coming to take us on the right." He marked these positions with his toe, then looked up. "The Army of North Virginia will have to fight well in the morning."

By the time night fell over the two armies, Jeff found himself so ill he couldn't even sit up. He was lying off to the side, Tom sitting beside him, and was barely aware as the men cooked their evening meal. They had obtained some beef for the first time since the march started. But the smell of it only made Jeff sicker.

"I don't know what's the matter with me," he muttered. His lips were dry, and his skin felt hot enough to crack.

"You'll be all right. As soon as the battle's over, we'll get you out of here," Tom said. In truth, he was worried about his younger brother. Dysentery and a host of other deadly ailments had killed men just as surely as if they'd been hit in the middle with a musket ball.

Tom moved over to sit beside Henry Mapes and said quietly, "I wish Jeff were back in Richmond. We've lost about as many to sickness like this as to men getting shot."

The sergeant turned his dark eyes on Jeff and shook his head. "It's a bad time for it, Tom. We'd better move him back tonight. Those blue-bellies might come earlier than we think."

"I'll take him back after the men eat."

Jeff was vaguely aware of what was going on. He had fallen into a fitful sleep, and then he heard a voice that he knew belonged to Jed Hawkins. He was singing a song called "Tenting Tonight," which was a favorite in his company. It had always been one of Jeff's favorites. He lay half concious as the words drifted across his mind.

"We're tenting tonight on the old camp ground,
Give us a song to cheer our weary hearts.
A song of home, and friends we love so dear.
Many are the hearts that are weary tonight,
Wishing for the war to cease,
Many are the hearts looking for the right
To see the dawn of peace.

"Tenting tonight, tenting tonight
Tenting on the old camp ground
Dying on the old camp ground."

Finally the voice grew muted. Then Jeff felt hands on him and heard Tom's voice.

"Come on, Jeff. We have to move you back out of this a little bit. We wouldn't want you to get caught in the battle in the morning."

Jeff was vaguely aware of struggling to his feet, and as he staggered from the field, he was lost in a fiery fever that seemed to scorch his very spirit.

9

The Bloodiest Day

Both the Carters and the Majorses would remember Wednesday, September 17, 1862, as the bloodiest day of the Civil War.

General McClellan with his overwhelming force could have won the battle if he had simply sent all of his men forward at once. The Confederate lines were so thin that they couldn't have held. If he had done so, the Army of Northern Virginia would have been destroyed, and the war would have ended shortly.

McClellan, however, did no such thing. He fed his men across the creek in small groups. This allowed General Lee to move the Confederates back and forth to meet these separate attacks.

The first assault came when General Hooker led his men through a thirty-acre cornfield.

Royal Carter was one of those men. He looked up as his company moved forward and saw that they were advancing into a line of guns.

"Look at those guns, Dave," he said. "They're going to cut us to pieces."

Dave Mellon's face grew pale. "They sure are, but there's no way out of it, Royal."

The two had been friends since childhood. They had gone fox hunting together, had courted the same girl at one time, and had fought over her and later made up. They had joined the army on the same day and had been together throughout the course of the war.

Now they marched together into battle. The muskets began to fire, and Dave said, "It sounds like giants breaking a bunch of sticks."

Royal had no time to answer, for suddenly the air was filled with screaming, whizzing shells. He saw men of his company begin to fall. Corporal Matlock suddenly was driven backward, and he fell loosely to the ground. Corporal Anderson screamed, "Close up ranks! Forward!" stepping into the fallen corporal's place.

Royal gritted his teeth as they advanced across the cornfield. There was no one for him to shoot at, for the Confederates were well hidden. All he knew was the sound of bullets flying, of men screaming, and then he saw Dave Mellon drop his musket and grab his chest.

"Dave!" Royal ran to him. When he rolled the young man over, he saw that Dave's chest was red and his eyes were glazing.

"Got me this time. Tell Mama that I died believing in Jesus."

Sergeant Ira Pickens was right behind Royal. He jerked him to his feet and said, "Come on, Royal. He's gone, and we're in trouble."

They were in trouble indeed, and before they left the cornfield there were so many blue-clad corpses on it that one Confederate said, "I could have walked across it on bluecoated bodies and never have touched the ground."

The battle raged on the left, and then General Sumner came roaring into the center. Some of the Stonewall Brigade had been moved to take the force of that action. Tom Majors and his company were part of that group. They began firing as rapidly as they could load and unload.

"I've never seen so many bluecoats in all my life," Curly Henson shouted. "There must be a million of them."

Tom said, "Be sure you don't miss. They're not going to stop." He loaded and fired and reloaded like a robot until the barrel was hot, but it was not enough. The overwhelming force of the Union attack kept coming.

He looked around to see his father, who was now firing from behind a log. There was no question of retreating. The Potomac River was behind them, so there was no place to go. Tom loaded his musket, his face black with powder, and fired again and again.

Far over on the right, General Burnside tried to drive his men across a narrow bridge. It was no more than twelve feet wide, and the Union troops who tried to fight their way across did not get far. Longstreet's men picked them off, and time after time the Northern soldiers had to retreat.

Then the Union troops gained a foothold, and finally it looked as though they would be able to win the battle. If they could take this position, they could swing around behind the rest of the long, crooked Rebel line.

"We're not going to be able to hold them!" a Confederate officer cried. At the same time a movement caught his eye. "Look! Who are those men? Are they ours or theirs?"

His fellow officer looked through his field glasses and then cried out, "It's A. P. Hill, here from Harper's Ferry!"

It was indeed General Hill of the Army of Northern Virginia. He'd marched his men hard, and now he threw them into the battle. It was this that saved the day for the Confederates. The breach was sealed, and the battle was over.

The sun went down, glowing blood red in the smoky twilight, and the light faded over the battlefield. Gradually the thunder of the guns died away. Then the musketry ceased too, and a silence came on, broken only by an occasional volley like the last drops of a shower. The bloodiest single day in all American history was finally over. Neither side knew exactly how many men it had lost. There was a truce to bury the dead and collect the wounded the next day.

The Army of Northern Virginia had never been in worse condition. The Federals held the cornfield and various river crossings, and Lee had lost a fourth of his army. His officers all urged him to retreat, but he remained in position all the next day.

McClellan, however, had had all the fighting he wanted. He had received fresh troops and now had enough men once again to win the battle, but such was beyond General McClellan.

Captain Nelson Majors was busy trying to pull together the shattered remnants of his company.

Jeff had been taken several hundred yards back, away from the line of battle. All day he heard the cannon roar and the crackle of muskets. But he was so ill he couldn't rise from the ground.

Finally, as the air cooled and the sun began to go down, his fever broke, and he gained some strength. Trembling in every nerve, he rose to his feet, his mind cloudy. He was determined to find his father and brother, so he stumbled along through the thickets. Unfortunately, he took a wrong turn and wound his way through a scrub forest.

Perhaps that was fortunate instead. If he had found his way to the battle, in all likelihood he would have been shot down, helpless as he was.

Now he stumbled once more and fell full-length on his face. "Got to get up . . ." he whispered hoarsely. "Got to find Pa and Tom." He struggled to his hands and knees, and as he rose the world seemed to go in a circle. He held onto a sapling until the dizziness passed and then staggered forward.

Jeff never knew how long he managed to keep on his feet, but the journey seemed unending. He fell more than once. His mind was so cloudy that he began speaking to his fellow soldiers as if they were there. "Curly, you're all right. Help me, will you? Sergeant Mapes, I can't find you. Where are you?" All this time he reeled forward, his face scratched from briars and low-hanging branches.

Finally he thought he heard voices, but he was too weak to walk toward them. Then his foot slipped under a root. He went crashing to the ground and with a sob tried to get up, but it was too much for him. As the thunder of the guns died away, Jeff Majors slipped into unconsciousness on the battlefield of Antietam.

"Tom, I can't find Jeff anywhere."

Captain Majors stopped beside his son, who, along with Walter Beddows, was digging a grave. "What do you mean you can't find him, Pa?" Tom said, forgetting to use his father's proper title. His face was pale, and his hands were trembling. He stared at the captain, saying, "He's got to be there."

"Well, he's not. Come on. Come with me. We'll have to find him."

Tom tossed the shovel down and followed his father quickly. "You think the Yankees got him?"

"Oh, he was too far behind our lines for that. But he's gone somewhere. I should've left someone with him."

"There really wasn't anyone to leave. But we'll find him—don't worry," Tom replied.

They searched for the rest of the afternoon. Finally word came that there was going to be a retreat across the Potomac.

"We can't leave him here, Pa. He's got to be somewhere," Tom cried.

"I know it. I'll see if I can get permission to stay."

Stonewall Jackson was a busy man that day. But he put aside everything to listen to Captain Majors. His eyes were filled with sympathy, but he said, "We have to get across the river, Captain. If you stay here, you'll be gobbled up as a prisoner of war again. If the boy's hurt, even if they find him, he'll be a prisoner at the worst."

"I don't want him to be in a prisoner of war camp, General Jackson!"

"Neither do I. But we'll have to trust God for this." It was the best Nelson Majors could do. He returned to the camp, and when the retreat started there was nothing to do but go with his men.

The Army of Northern Virginia pulled up at the Potomac that night. The men struggled across, and one of the last groups to cross over was the

Stonewall Brigade. As they moved wearily across the river, Tom looked back where the Union Army lay, still inactive.

"I sure hate to leave Jeff here. I surely hate to do it," he muttered under his breath. He lowered his head and joined the troops, and soon they were across the river, safe from attack by the Federal Army.

They were leaving behind many who would never fight again. The countryside would be filled with graves, some single and sometimes twenty men buried in a mass grave. Lee's attack on the North had failed. Both armies were cut to pieces, but while the North had men to fill the gaps left by the battle, the South had none.

Nelson Majors ruefully observed, "We're surely going to be spread mighty thin from now on!"

10

"I Can't Go Home"

Royal! Thank God! You're all right!"

Leah had been watching the line of stretcher-bearers bringing the wounded back from the battle. She was so intent on searching the faces on the stretchers that at first she didn't see her brother staggering along beside them. When she saw him, she gasped, only then realizing that her worst fears had been groundless.

She ran to Royal and, throwing her arms around him, held him tightly, her eyes shut to keep the tears back.

Royal held his sister, stroking her long blonde hair. When he stepped back, she saw that his eyes were red with fatigue and black with gunpowder.

"I'm fine, sis," he said. "Not a scratch."

"What about the others?" Leah asked, almost afraid to hear the answer. "Are—are our own boys all right?"

"We lost some—but Ira's all right."

Leah squeezed her eyes shut once again, not daring to ask which boys from their own valley would never return to its green peacefulness. "Come on, Royal," she finally urged. "Pa wanted to see you as soon as I found you. You can tell us both about it."

"How is he?"

"Not good. He's not sleeping, but he has no

strength to get up, and I don't know what else to do for him."

The two found Dan Carter sitting with his back against a tree. As soon as he saw Royal, his eyes lit up and from somewhere he mustered the strength to struggle to his feet. "God be thanked!" he exclaimed, putting his arms around the young soldier. "You're safe!"

"Sure am, Pa." Royal smiled, obviously making light of the horror he had experienced in order to spare his father. "I guess your prayers—and Leah's —are pretty strong."

"You look beat out, son," Mr. Carter said. "I'm sure your spirit's as tuckered out as your body after the hell you went through today. Sit down and take something to eat."

Royal responded to his father's offer. "I'm not very hungry, Pa, but I just can't get enough to drink."

Leah pushed him over to a shady spot. "You sit down right there, Royal!" As soon as he slumped down next to his father, who in turn slid down the tree trunk to rest beside him, Leah scurried around, bringing him a big tin cup of water, then stirring up the fire. Soon the air was filled with the smell of bacon frying, and when she put a plateful of bacon and beans in front of him, he ate hungrily.

"I'm eating like a hog!" he exclaimed. His mouth was blackened from the black-powder cartridges he had ripped open with his teeth in the scurry to reload during the battle. "Fellow forgets all about fine manners in a battle—and afterward too."

"Don't you be worrying about manners, Royal," Leah said. "Nothing a clean wet rag and some soap can't fix. I'll fix you some coffee," she continued, "and then you can wash up out of the wash tin over on that barrel by the wagon." Soon she returned the tin cup, this time full of steaming, strong black coffee.

"Got any sugar for this?" he asked.

"Oh, I forgot!" She ran and came back with a small canful. "The only times I've known you to take sugar in your coffee was when you were plumb tuckered out from clearing land for plowing, or butchering." She thrust the sugar tin toward him.

When Royal had shoveled five large spoonfuls into his cup, she found a smile. "You just drink coffee to get all that sugar," she chuckled. Then she sat down and drew her knees up. "Tell us about the battle, Royal."

"It was the worst yet. I pray to God I never see worse." He spoke of the charge he'd made through the cornfield, and how men had gone down on both sides of him. "It was like they were cut down with a scythe," he murmured.

"And you just kept going?"

"As far as we could. But we took a licking in that field. When we had to retreat, our fellows were all over the ground. Lots of 'em were wounded, but the Rebs captured the ones that weren't too bad off. They just left the really bad ones."

Dan Carter sat with his eyes half shut, listening to Royal describe the battle. When his son's voice finally trailed off, he said simply, "I'm glad you're safe, son."

Royal gave his father and sister an odd look. He had a haunted look in his fine eyes as he said, "I don't think I'll ever forget this battle. So many of our fellows shot down!"

"Did we win, Royal?" Leah asked. She had listened to his story with a strange, sick feeling. As the long line of the wounded had passed, it had brought the terrible price of the war home to her.

"I guess so. In a way."

Dan looked at his son, frowning. "But we kept Lee and his army fought off, didn't we?"

"Pa, we should have captured the whole Army of Northern Virginia. We had the men to do it. The Rebs were stretched so thin—if we'd all gone at them, we'd have done it. And who knows but it might've marked the end of the war!"

"Why didn't you all go on?" Dan asked.

"General McClellan—they say he's good at training soldiers—but he's no fighting general. Just can't stand to send men into a battle."

"So we'll have to do it again?" Leah asked in horror.

Royal nodded wearily. "I'm afraid so. It's going to be a long war. The Rebs won't quit, and we can't whup 'em until we get us a fighting general!"

All afternoon Leah stayed busy taking water to the wounded. A steady stream of stretcher-bearers and ambulances flowed by on the road, and the men were all thirsty, it seemed. A creek ran through a grove of pecan trees two hundred yards from the road. How many times Leah made the trip carrying two buckets, she never knew. Her arms grew weary, but as the soldiers whispered their thanks, she felt it was little enough to do.

One young soldier with a bloody bandage on his arm stooped and drank thirstily, then managed a smile. "That was 'bout the best drink I ever had, miss." He was pale and looked terribly tired. Something in his face reminded Leah of Jeff.

"Where are you from?" Leah asked as she dipped more water into his cup.

"Virginia—just outside of Richmond."

Leah stared at him with surprise. "Why, I didn't expect to find any soldiers from there!"

"My folks didn't hold with slavery. When the war started, we left home and moved to the North."

Leah paused, thinking of Jeff and his family—only they had moved from Kentucky to Virginia to fight for states' rights. "That must have been hard for you. What's your name?"

"George Hill." He asked her name, then said, "Yes, it was sure hard to leave. It was the only home I knew."

Leah handed him the cup, saying, "I have an uncle who lives in Richmond. His name is Silas Carter."

"Don't guess I know him, Miss Leah. You ever visit him?"

"Oh, yes. My sister and I went there to take care of him."

"He's sick, is he?"

"He was, but he's better now."

"Where 'bouts does your uncle live?" He listened as Leah described the location of Silas's farm, and his eyes opened wide. "Why, I know that place. Been by it lots of time on the way to town."

"Is that right? Well, it's a small world, isn't it, George?"

The youthful soldier talked about his home, finally saying, "Don't guess I can ever go back there, even if we win this war."

"Why not?"

"Oh, everyone around there is for the South. You saw that, didn't you?"

"Yes, I guess I did," Leah nodded reluctantly. "But lots of them aren't for slavery either—they just don't think the federal government should have the say-so about it. Don't you think that if we win the war, they'll soften up?"

"After the war all our old neighbors will be thinking of my family as the ones who left to fight for the Yankees—the ones who took away their rights and killed their menfolks."

Leah was silent, for she had not thought of this. Then she said, "God brought you through this battle, George. He'll take care of you."

On impulse she touched his good arm and then motioned toward the wagon. She couldn't get Jeff out of her mind. "Why don't you come over and rest for a while? I'll fix you something to eat."

George brightened and went with her. While Leah was fixing a simple meal as she had earlier for her brother, her father sat and talked with the young soldier. When Leah brought a plate of food, he ate hungrily, then handed back the plate. "That was fine, Miss Leah!"

"Let me wash that wound a little, and then you can take a little nap. You'll feel better."

"Reckon that might be good. I don't want infection, and I'm tuckered out."

When the soldier had gone to lie down on a blanket underneath a tree, Leah told her father about him. "He can't ever go back to Virginia, Pa," she said sadly. "I can't think of much worse than not ever going home."

Dan Carter stroked his scraggly mustache slowly. "Another bad thing about this war," he muttered. "Even when the shooting is over, there'll still be lots of grief."

117

Leah kept at her station, giving water to the endless line of soldiers.

And then George Hill came to say good-bye. "Thanks for everything, Miss Leah," he said. "I'd better get going."

"I hope everything works out for you, George." She smiled thinly.

"Well, I'll have one good memory of Antietam." George grinned. "I can't go home again, but I'll never forget a pretty young lady taking time to give me water and a meal. Thanks, and good-bye."

As Leah watched him go, Ezra came to stand beside her. He'd spent the hours since the battle helping the camp's chief surgeon sort out the casualties. He watched the young soldier stride off, both arms swinging equally, almost as if he hadn't been wounded. "I guess he'll be all right. That wound's not too bad."

Leah shook her head. "But he's so sad, Ezra. Virginia was his home, and now he can't ever go back there."

"But he's alive, and he's got a family. He'll be all right."

Leah turned and exclaimed, "You've always got a home with us, Ezra."

"I think about that quite a bit." He looked at the line of wounded and the ambulances and said quietly, "Nothing's worth much in this world unless you have people. I ain't never had any, so I know about that."

At supper that night, Ezra noticed that Leah said almost nothing. She went to bed early, and he cleaned up the dishes. When he was finished, he sat

118

down beside Dan Carter and asked, "How are you feeling, sir?"

"Well, not as well as I'd like, but I'm asking God for strength to keep on. It helps a heap to know Royal's all right."

"You sure handed out a bunch of tracts and Bibles today by Leah's never-empty water barrel."

Carter hadn't the strength to dip the water for the thirsty soldiers, but every soldier who got water from Leah got a tract from him. "I wish I could give a Bible to all of them," he said finally. "Poor boys—all wounded and some of them not going to make it!"

Ezra's brow wrinkled, and he said hesitantly, "Leah didn't say five words at supper—and then went right off to bed. I sure hope she ain't getting sick."

"I think she's worried about Jeff."

"I reckon you're right."

"She thinks a heap of that boy," Dan murmured. "They grew up like brother and sister." He glanced at Ezra, then asked, "She say anything to you about the set-to she had with him?"

"Just a little."

"Well, it don't take much to upset Leah where Jeff's concerned. Wish it hadn't happened. She can't help but think how bad it would be if he got killed. She'd never forgive herself if that happened."

"It would be downright hard on her, wouldn't it?"

"Yes. Bad enough to have a fight—but to have no chance to ask for forgiveness—can't think of much worse than that!"

"I guess Sarah is pretty upset about Tom. I

mean, she knows he's with Lee. And here's her brother, Royal, going right up against him."

"She won't talk much about it, but she's heart-sick over the war and all the tearing up of people it's caused."

Ezra shook his head sadly. "I was in poor shape in that prison camp. All I thought about was my own misery. Now I'm out and healthy and not in the army, so I won't be in any battles." He ran his hand through his curly brown hair in a gesture of frustration. "But since I became a Christian, I'm seeing that other people hurt pretty bad."

"Why, I guess that's part of knowing Jesus," Mr. Carter said. "We're born selfish, and it takes a touch from God to cause us to think of others."

Ezra grinned suddenly. "Fellow asked me once, 'If you had your picture took with ten other fellows, when you got to see the picture, who'd be the first one you'd look for?' And I said I'd look for me."

"I guess we'd all do that."

"I bet you wouldn't, Mr. Carter. If you had a picture of your family, I'll bet you'd look for your wife or one of the children first."

Dan Carter laughed. "I hope so, Ezra, but I'm not so sure."

They sat talking for an hour, neither one of them daring to further voice his deepest concern about Leah. What if Jeff had died during the battle?

Mr. Carter's energy faded visibly over the hour, and finally he said, his voice thin and tired, "Guess I'll get to bed." He got to his feet slowly, but then halted and said suddenly, "If anything happens to me, Ezra, you'll take care of Leah?"

Startled, Ezra looked hard at the older man. "Why, sure—but you'll be all right."

"I hope so. But a day like today starts a man thinking about his own end, especially when he's feeling poorly. It's good knowing that you're here to take care of things. I've come to lean on you a lot, Ezra. I think God sent you to be a part of our family."

Ezra flushed. "I've never had folks before. Sure am glad God sent me your way."

After Dan Carter had climbed into the wagon, Ezra sat for a long time thinking of how he'd come to this place in his life. Finally he said quietly, "God, You've sure been good to me!"

Just a few miles away, across Antietam Creek, Jeff lay on his back, burning with fever again. He would awaken at times, struggle to his feet, and try to walk.

"Got . . . to find . . . Pa!" he mumbled, but the woods were thick with saplings that caught at him and roots that caused him to stumble. He had vivid dreams, but when he fell into a feverish sleep, it seemed that the whole world went dark.

When he recovered enough to look around, he saw no one and knew a moment of bleak despair. "Can't find my way . . ." he muttered.

He finally lay down beside a large tree and began to pray. "God . . . I can't do anything . . . please . . . send somebody to help me . . . please!"

Overhead, the stars burned in the velvet sky. A part of the moon appeared, sending pale gleams down on the still form of Jeff Majors. Once a fox came out of the wood and sniffed at the boy, then leaped back and disappeared into the dense woods.

11

"Why, Thee Is Only a Boy!"

Amos Golden was a Quaker. He had lived in Sharpsburg all of his life and knew everyone, not only in town but on every farm in a thirty-mile radius. Now as he stood outside his farmhouse door, he wondered if he would ever be able to forget what had happened the previous day.

"What is thee staring at, Father?"

Golden turned to find his older daughter, Ann, watching him.

She was a tall young woman with black hair and dark blue eyes. She came to stand beside him, and together they looked toward the rolling hills where the battle had taken place the day before.

Golden said simply, "I'm grieved, daughter, over the terrible ways that men treat each other."

"It is a terrible thing." Ann nodded. The two of them stood staring out into the afternoon air. The sun was high, and they could see clearly the moving forms of soldiers in the distance. "What are they doing?" she asked.

"Tending the wounded and burying the dead," Golden said shortly.

Ann Golden shook her head. "What a pity! So many fine young men gone for nothing."

As a Quaker, Golden did not believe in war. He had no sons, but he had four daughters, and now he wondered what he would've done if his sons had been in the battle. Suddenly a thought came to him, and he turned to face his daughter, his blue eyes intent. "Something comes to me, Ann."

"Yes, what is it, Father?"

"Maybe some of those men will die if they don't get help. I think I'll go see if we can offer any assistance."

Ann turned to her mother inside the house. "Thee had better get ready, Mother. Father is going to see if he can help the wounded. It wouldn't surprise me if he didn't bring some of them here."

That indeed was on Amos's mind. However, when he reached the battlefield he grew so sickened by the sight that he almost faltered. Nevertheless he found his way to one of the rough field hospitals and watched as the doctors did their best for the wounded men. Their best, he saw, was not a great deal. Those who'd had arms or legs shattered by musket balls immediately had them amputated.

Amos wandered around until finally a surgeon wearing a bloody apron noticed him. "What's your purpose, sir?" he demanded.

"Does thee need help?" Amos asked quietly.

"Are you a doctor?"

"No, I'm a farmer."

The surgeon unfortunately had been working all day trying to save as many men as he could. His temper was short, and he snapped, "You civilians run away when the battle starts, and then you come around asking if you can help when it's over. Be off with you!"

Golden did not reply. He was a meek man and had never been in a fight in his life. He had learned long ago to control his temper. He walked away to do his best to help the wounded without permission. He found many of them suffering from thirst.

Finding pots and canteens, he went to the river and spent the afternoon offering water to the thirsty men.

Many of them he saw were very young. For these he felt special compassion. One young boy, no more than fifteen or sixteen, was obviously dying. Golden stayed with him for a long time murmuring encouragement, moistening his lips with water, and finally praying for him when he could do nothing else.

The boy looked up once and whispered, "I'm going to die, ain't I?"

"We all have to do that," Amos said gently.

"I'm only sixteen. I haven't even lived, and now I've got to die. I'm afraid!"

"Thee need not be afraid, my boy," Amos said. "The good Lord will receive you to Himself. Do you know the Lord?"

"No—no, I didn't never pay attention to God."

Amos pulled out a thick New Testament from his waistband and for more than an hour read Scripture after Scripture to the dying boy. From time to time he would encourage him, saying, "Put your trust in the Lord Jesus. He died for thee."

The boy's life slipped away slowly. He held the big thick hand of the farmer, clinging to it as if it were life, and finally prayed to God for forgiveness.

"That's good. That's good, my boy," Amos whispered. Ten minutes later the lad slipped out to meet his Savior.

Amos folded the boy's hands, searched through his pockets, and found a Philadelphia address. He copied it down, saying, "I will write your people, my boy, and tell them you died believing in Jesus."

The earth seemed to be pressing in on Jeff. His head seemed to weigh as much as a bale of cotton when he tried to lift it. His lips were pressed down into the dirt, and he could taste sand and grit. Finally he rolled over onto his back. The sun was going down, and it made a huge red wafer in the sky that almost blinded him. His lips were so dry he could not speak, and his tongue felt as thick as his arm.

"Got to get up . . . got to get help!" he croaked and managed to get to his hands and knees. He trembled so badly that he knew he'd never be able to stand erect, so he tried to crawl. Once he tried to call out, but no one came. *I'm going to die,* he thought and fell flat once again, lying face down on the earth.

He never knew how long he lay there, but then he heard footsteps and managed to call in a strange, croaking voice, "Help . . . help me!"

Then Jeff felt strong hands. He felt himself being pulled into a sitting position. He blinked, opened his eyes, and saw the round, reddish face of a man with a full beard looking at him. His voice, when it came, seemed to come from far away.

"Why, thee is only a boy!" the voice said.

Jeff whispered, "Help me! Don't let the Yankees get me!"

Golden had no political opinions, except that all men should love one another. He saw that this soldier was very ill indeed and, reaching down, he put his arms under the boy's knees and lifted him up. He was a strong man and bore his burden to a creek that wound through the trees. There he put the soldier down and dipped his handkerchief in the water. He wiped the boy's burning face, and the lad cried out, "Water!"

Amos had nothing to hold water with except his hands, and he made a cup of them. The young soldier drank, and the water seemed to refresh him a little. His lips became less tight. "Who won the battle?" he whispered.

"That I cannot tell thee," Amos said. He suspected from the boy's tattered rags that he was a Confederate, for the Union soldiers wore neat blue uniforms. "Thee is part of Lee's army, I take it?"

"Yes." The soldier nodded. "Don't let the Yankees have me. I'd rather die than go to prison."

Amos Golden looked down, and a resolution formed in his head. "I will take thee home," he said. "Then we'll ask the Lord what to do."

Reaching down, Golden picked the young man up again. He had to stop three times on the way home, for the boy was not a light burden. Finally, however, just as darkness completely fell, he walked up to the front door of his own house.

"Father, who hast thee brought us?" his wife asked.

"One who needs help," Golden answered. He moved inside and walked into the only bedroom. He lay the boy, who was now unconscious, on the quilt-covered bed and looked around at his family. "God has given us a task. We will do our best for the one He has sent. He will need care, but I feel that God will be with him."

Jeff finally awoke from a sound sleep, his head aching. The sun was shining through the window, and it blinded him. As he moved, he heard a voice say, "Thee is awake."

126

Jeff looked quickly at the woman who stood by the bed, a young girl beside her. He was frightened, not knowing where he was, and he tried to speak. "Where—where is this place?" he whispered.

"Thee is safe," the woman said. "My name is Martha Golden. This is my daughter, Ann."

Jeff stared at them. "How did I get here?"

"My husband found thee in the woods. He brought thee here last night."

Jeff tried to sit up, and the woman helped him. "Here. I will get thee some food. Ann, thee must watch him."

The woman left the room, and the tall, black-haired girl asked, "What is thy name?"

Jeff stared at her and swallowed. "Jeff. Jeff Majors. Why do you talk so funny?"

The girl smiled at him. "We are Friends," she said.

"Friends?" Jeff asked, surprised. "But I never saw you before."

"No, I mean we are 'Friends'—you might know us as 'Quakers.' We always say *thee* and *thou*—it is respectful. And we do not believe in war."

Jeff stared at her, his head still swimming. "I don't believe in it much myself," he said. He looked down and saw that he was wearing a white gown of some kind, and he stared back at the girl, wondering how he'd gotten bathed and in bed.

At that moment, Mrs. Golden came in with a bowl of soup. Just the smell of it made Jeff hungry.

"Here. Thee must eat. When did thee eat last?"

"Day before yesterday, I think." Jeff ate the soup and, as soon as he finished, felt terribly sleepy. "Don't know what's wrong with me . . . ." And then he fell over to one side, sound asleep.

"Is he dead?" Ann whispered.

"No. Just worn out. He'll be all right." Mrs. Golden went to her husband, who was sitting in the kitchen, and said, "He ate something."

Amos drew a sigh of relief. "I feared he might die, he had so much fever."

"He's still very weak. He might die yet."

"No. God has brought him here. We will care for him, and we will see that he gets back to his people."

Jeff awakened later in the day and found the big man sitting beside him. "I remember you," he said. "You found me in the woods."

"Yes. How does thee feel?"

Jeff coughed. "Terrible! My bones hurt, and I'm on fire."

"Thee has a bad sickness."

Jeff said, "You won't turn me over to the Yankees, will you?"

"They may come looking," Golden said. "I could not lie if they ask if we're harboring anyone."

As sick as he was, Jeff's mind worked quickly. "Will you do one thing for me?"

"If I can, lad."

"Go to the Union lines. Ask for a sutler named Dan Carter. Don't talk to anyone else. Tell him that I'm here. Tell him Jeff Majors is here. Will you do that for me?"

Amos Golden stroked his beard thoughtfully, his eyes on the boy, and finally he said, "What would a Yankee sutler do for *thee*?"

"We're close friends. He's almost like a second father to me. He'll help me. Take care of me."

Amos Golden looked at the boy and nodded slowly. "Yes. If he's to be found, I'll find him."

He rose and left the room, and Jeff began to pray. "O God, let him find the Carters. Don't let me go to prison—I couldn't stand that!"

12

Council of War

He doesn't seem to be getting any better, Leah. I'm plumb worried about him."

Leah stared at Ezra, her troubled face echoing his words. Her father had gotten steadily worse since the battle.

"I think we'd better get him home as quick as we can," she agreed. "If he can stand the hard trip." She was worried, and her face showed it. "Maybe we can get some farm family to take us in here until he gets better or rent a room or something like that."

"Maybe." Ezra scratched his chin thoughtfully. "Might be a little hard to do. People are pretty standoffish, what with the battle and all."

"I sent a letter to Ma, but I don't know how long it'll take to get there. And I don't know what good it'll do, because she can't come here anyhow and leave Esther alone. We'd better start back right away."

"All right. The animals are in good shape," Ezra said. "I'll grain them extra good tonight. We'll start home first thing in the morning."

The two of them went about their chores then. They'd distributed all of their supplies to the soldiers, so the wagon was practically empty. Leah had moved her father back into her cot inside the wagon, and now she used some of the last of their provisions to cook supper.

She had seen enough of the wounded to disturb her dreams for the rest of her life and had wept over the death of Dave Mellon. He had been a friend for so long it was hard to believe that he was gone. She was grateful that Royal had been spared. He had come to her the day after the battle and told her about Dave's death and the loss of two other boys from Pineville. Now as she fixed supper, she could not help but think about them.

She finished the cooking and called out, "Ezra, why don't you come and tend this meat while I take Pa something?"

Even as she spoke, a man came walking out of the falling darkness into the camp. He was a big, heavy man with a full beard and a pair of steady blue eyes.

"Yes, sir, can I help you?" Leah asked.

"I'm looking for a sutler named Dan Carter."

"I'm Leah Carter. Dan Carter's my father, but he's ill right now."

Her words seemed to trouble the visitor. He stood uncertainly, looked down at the ground, and stroked his beard thoughtfully. "Is he bad ill, does thee say?"

"I'm afraid so. We're taking him home first thing in the morning."

"My name is Amos Golden."

"Do you know my father, Mr. Golden?"

"No, lass, I don't."

"I'll see if he's awake."

Leah walked to the rear of the wagon, lifted up the canvas and said, "Pa, are you awake?"

"Yes, I am." His voice was thin and tired but also determined.

Leah turned to the stranger and said, "Mr. Golden, he's awake if you'd like to talk to him."

Amos Golden walked to the wagon and looked inside, though it was too dark to see anything. He cleared his throat and asked quietly, "Is thee Daniel Carter?"

"Yes, I am."

"I'm sorry to hear thee is ill," he said. "Not harmed in the battle, I hope?"

"No." Dan Carter got up from his cot and came to the edge of the wagon. He awkwardly sat down so that he could see the face of the visitor. "What can I do for you?"

Golden again hesitated. He lowered his voice and said, "I have a message for thee."

"A message? From who?"

"A young man. He says his name is Jeff Majors."

Leah had been close enough to hear. She came at once and said, "Jeff Majors? Oh, where is he?"

"At my house. He's in pretty bad shape."

"Was he wounded?" Leah demanded instantly.

"No, lass. He's sick. I think he was sick before the battle started, or so he said anyway. He's too weak to move."

"What's the message?" Dan Carter inquired.

Golden looked suddenly at Ezra, who had come closer. He turned back to Dan, saying, "Is it all right to speak freely?"

"Yes, you can say anything in front of these two."

"Very well. The young man says he is afraid of being taken prisoner by the Federal Army. He asked if thee will help him get to his home."

A silence fell for a moment, and then Dan said,

"Well, we'll do all we can, of course. He's a good friend of ours."

"I don't know," Golden said slowly. "He's in bad shape . . ."

"I understand, but God will make a way."

At that Golden smiled. "Thee is a Christian man. That's good." He hesitated, then said, "I fear the Federals will begin searching the houses for escaped Confederates. Already they've questioned my neighbors. If they come, I wouldn't be able to lie to them."

Leah said, "We've got to get him, Father. We can't let him go to prison. He'd die there!"

"That's right," Ezra said quickly. "I don't reckon our Yankee prisons are any better than the one I was in in Virginia. We'll have to get him."

Dan Carter thought for a moment. But he was so weak that it seemed he couldn't think clearly, and he said, "You two will have to handle it. I can't help, but I can pray." Then he turned to the big man, saying, "I thank you, sir, for your kindness. God will bless you for it."

Golden nodded. "I will pray that God will give thee strength, friend Carter. What does thee wish me to do?"

"Can we drive the wagon right up to your house?" Leah asked.

"Why, yes. That would be no trouble at all. I will show thee the way. It isn't far."

Ezra said, "It will take about half an hour to get ready and break camp. I'll hitch the team, Leah. You just throw everything we've got into the wagon. We've got to move fast."

Leah did move fast, and by the time Ezra had the team hitched, she had all their belongings in

133

the wagon. She hurriedly scribbled a good-bye note to Royal and tacked it to the tree their wagon had been hitched under. They had already said their farewells earlier in the day, since Royal's army duties would have prevented him from seeing them off in the morning.

"I'm ready," she said. "If you'll show us the way, Mr. Golden."

"This way, lass."

Jeff was asleep, but as soon as he heard a voice he opened his eyes. "Jeff?" the familiar voice said, and when he was able to focus, he whispered, "Leah, it's you."

Leah bent over him. "Yes." She put her hand on his forehead and said, "You're burning up with fever."

"I know, but I've got to get out of here." He shifted his head and saw Ezra coming into the room, followed by Amos Golden. "Ezra, help me."

"Why, sure I will, Jeff. Me and Leah, we'll get you out of this." He turned to Golden. "I reckon we'd better take him right now."

"If the patrol stops thee, thee may have trouble. Maybe all would be held and tried as spies."

"We've been in trouble before, the three of us." Ezra grinned and winked at Jeff. "Get ready for a little trip," he said.

"Let me put on my clothes," Jeff pleaded. "I can't go in this nightgown!"

"Thy clothes are too ragged to wear," Golden protested. "And mine are too big for thee."

"You can wear some of mine, Jeff," Ezra said. "I'll go get them."

Jeff was so weak he hardly knew what was going on. He was aware that Ezra had taken over and had sent Leah from the room with the women. He tried to help with the clothes, but he was so frail he could do little.

But soon Ezra had him fully dressed. "Can you stand up to walk?"

"We can take him," Golden said. "I carried thee in my arms once—now I will do it again." Without further ado, he stooped over and in his mighty arms picked the boy up. Jeff's head bobbed as the big man carried him outside and laid him on the pallet of soft blankets Leah had made in the wagon, next to the cot that held her father.

Dan Carter greeted him warmly. "Jeff," he said in a sick man's voice, "looks like the two of us are going to make a hospital. But we'll make it all right."

The Goldens came into the yard, and Jeff thanked them all.

Then Amos said, "Thee had better stick to the back roads for a while."

Leah climbed up on the seat beside Ezra and cried out, "Thank you. Thank you so much, all of you."

"Thee is welcome, daughter. We will pray for the young man and thy father."

Soon the wagon was trundling down a rough road.

The air was silent, but Leah and Ezra were tense.

"The cavalry sometimes sends out patrols on roads like this to pick up deserters. Sure would hate to meet any," Ezra said.

However they were fortunate, and two or three hours later Ezra drew up the team, and the two of them climbed into the wagon.

"You all right, Jeff?" Ezra asked.

Jeff nodded weakly. "Just get me home."

Leah said, "Pa, I don't know what to do. You need to get home to Kentucky. Jeff needs to go to Virginia. We can't do both."

Dan Carter was lying still on his bunk. The rough road had shaken him, and he must have felt almost as bad as Jeff. However, he lifted his head and smiled. "I've been wanting to see my Uncle Silas for a long time—and it looks like the time has come for me to do it. Take us to Virginia, Ezra."

Ezra looked at the two sick men and nodded. "Yes, sir. I'll sure do that. Just lie there and take it easy. With God's help, we'll make it fine!"

13

Ezra Earns His Keep

The journey from Sharpsburg was difficult for the travelers. The countryside swarmed with Federal patrols, for many Confederates were still trapped on the east side of the Potomac. Some had been too badly wounded to make the journey across the river, while others had gotten separated from their units. As the wagon was driven down the back roads, Ezra kept a lookout for Union patrols. Several times he spotted them coming by the dust clouds their horses kicked up, and he managed to pull off into the shelter of the thickets. Early on the second day, however, he was taken by surprise. "Look! There's a Federal patrol coming."

Leah looked ahead to where Ezra pointed. A troop of some fifteen cavalry had rounded the bend ahead of them.

"What do we do, Ezra? It's too late to hide."

"Let me do the talking," Ezra said quickly. He leaned back and said loudly enough for the two sick men to hear him, "Federal cavalry ahead. You fellows just keep your heads down, and we'll be all right."

Leah watched with apprehension as the lieutenant in charge of the troop threw up his hand and brought the patrol to a stop. The horses chuffed and pawed the dust, and the lieutenant eyed them sharply. He was a small man with a bushy cavalry mustache and tawny hair that fell over his shoulders in a very unmilitary manner. Leah thought he must have been influenced by the Union general George Armstrong Custer, who—she had heard—wore his hair in such an outlandish fashion.

"What's your business?" the lieutenant snapped in a high-pitched tone. He rode a large black horse and pulled back cruelly on the bit as the animal tried to buck.

"That's a spirited horse you've got there, Lieutenant," Ezra said quickly. "Ain't never seen a finer one."

The lieutenant seemed pleased by Ezra's remark. "There's not any better," he said. "Finest cavalry mount in the whole United States Army." He relaxed in his saddle and stared at Leah, who was wearing a pair of men's overalls for the journey.

She also wore a white shirt, and her blonde hair caught the sunlight. "Is the battle all over, Lieutenant?" she asked innocently.

"Sure is, miss. We whupped the daylights out of the Rebs! Run them clean back to Richmond," he announced proudly. Then he cleared his throat and assumed a more businesslike expression. "You're headed straight for Rebel territory, you know. What's your business?"

"Well, Lieutenant," Ezra said. "We've got a couple of sick men in here. They got the fever. They could use a doctor."

The lieutenant studied Ezra, then said, "I'll have to take a look in that wagon. Got lots of Rebs trying to make their way back South."

"Oh, that'll be fine, Lieutenant," Leah said at once. "Come along."

The lieutenant dismounted and handed the

reins to a grizzled sergeant, then advanced to the rear of the wagon.

Leah jumped to the ground and walked beside him.

He was a small man, no taller than she, and he straightened as though to make himself appear taller.

Leah drew back the cover of the wagon and said, "Pa, are you awake?"

Dan Carter raised himself to a sitting position on the cot that Ezra had fastened firmly to the floor. "Yes, I'm awake, daughter." He looked over at Jeff. "Son, you awake?"

Jeff still had a high fever and had been awakened by the stopping of the wagon. Now he lifted himself on one elbow and peered drearily at the end of the wagon, where Leah stood with the cavalry officer. "Yeah, I'm awake," he mumbled. "What is it?"

The lieutenant stared at the two men, bent over to assure himself that there were no other inhabitants, then said brusquely, "Checking for Rebs, mister. Sorry to have disturbed you. I think there is a doctor on up at Jessieville. Looks like you best get there as quick as you can." He stepped back from the wagon, probably breathing a sigh of relief that he hadn't gotten close to the infected men, and Leah closed the canvas covering. "Sorry to be a bother, miss," he said.

Leah smiled at him, her green eyes taking him in fully. "Oh, that's all right, Lieutenant. I know you're just doing your job, but we are worried about my folks."

The lieutenant twirled his mustache. He was somewhat of a dandy, no more than eighteen years old. "Maybe I'll check in later at Jessieville just to see how your folks are doing," he suggested.

Leah thought quickly and said, "That'll be fine, Lieutenant. We'll all be glad to see you."

The lieutenant grinned, went back to his horse, and swung into his saddle. "Forward!" he shouted as if he were leading a charge across the battlefield.

Leah and Ezra watched the patrol thunder down the road, and Ezra turned to grin at her. "Well, that was kind of fun, wasn't it?"

"Yes, it was," she said slowly. "But I don't think I want to have many more adventures like that."

Leah climbed back up into the wagon seat, Ezra said, "Giddap," and the horses started plodding along.

"That lieutenant might check with the doctor in Jessieville," she said. "That might be a little dangerous."

"I hadn't thought of that. Maybe it'd be best to stop. It wouldn't hurt to have the doctor look at them anyway. Neither one of them is doing too well."

They hurried on and did manage to find the doctor. He was busy with wounded men, but, after looking Dan and Jeff over, had both good news and bad. He was a middle-aged man, short and spare, with a pair of light blue eyes. "I don't know what it is they've got," he said. "Not cholera and not scarlet fever. Looks like trail fever."

"What's that?" Ezra demanded.

"Well, nobody knows exactly, but when the folks take the trail to California they just get fever. Nobody knows what it is."

"Can you give them anything for it?" Leah asked.

"No, just bed rest, water, and lots of prayer."

"We'll do that." Leah smiled. She reached into her purse and paid the doctor's fee, and then they went back to the wagon.

When they were on their way again, she said, "Well, if that lieutenant checks, he'll know we stopped here anyway."

"Reckon that's right. But I'm going to get off this main road. Don't want to be stopped again if we can help it."

They traveled slowly for the next three days, making no more than ten or fifteen miles a day. Each afternoon Ezra would find a creek and pull the wagon off the road out of sight. He usually disappeared then and came back bearing a chicken or a turkey. Once he came back with an armload of sausage and pigs' feet.

"Pigs' feet!" Leah turned up her nose. "I wouldn't eat those things!"

"Why, they're the best part of a pig," Ezra said as his eyes glinted with humor. "Except for the lips, that is. I couldn't get any of those; they were already gone. The good parts always go first."

Leah stared at him. "Pig *lips!*" She shuddered. "I'd just as soon eat snails!"

"I heard those Frenchmen eat snails and like them real good," he teased.

Leah sniffed. "Well, you know those foreigners —they'll eat *anything.*" She took the sausage and said, "We'll eat this and the eggs we have left. Maybe that'll do till we get something better."

That night Mr. Carter seemed to feel better,

but Jeff had not improved. He got out of the wagon, though, aided by Ezra, and sat with his back against a wheel. Ezra built up a small fire and made coffee. Jeff drank a cup, saying nothing.

Dan Carter looked across the fire and said, "Feeling a little peaked, are you, son?"

"I'll be all right," Jeff said. His voice was thin and weak, and his cheeks were sunken in, as were his eyes. He'd never been sick to speak of in his life, and now his physical illness seemed to have dragged him down emotionally as well.

Ezra kept the talk going around the campfire. He was a cheerful young man. From time to time, though, Jeff was able to trace some of the hardships Ezra had endured as a child. He'd never complained about them, but Jeff knew it had been terrible.

"I've been thinking about clearing those ten acres over by Bolton's creek, Mr. Carter," he said, tipping his coffee cup to his mouth to drain the last drops. "That's good land down there."

"That land would be hard. Those walnut trees are a hundred years old, I guess, Ezra."

"I know. We could sell them off and burn the stumps, and when we get them pulled out that would be a good place to grow sorghum. Maybe we could do that like your Uncle Silas."

"I don't think sorghum grows well in the North," Dan said. "But we could sure put some winter wheat in there, or maybe feed for the cows." The two men went on talking about the farm, and Leah sat down beside Jeff.

"I'm sorry you feel so bad," she said.

Jeff nodded. He tried to think of something to say, but he'd never been able to get over the way

142

he'd treated Leah when he left. He knew that he ought to simply say he was sorry, but somehow he couldn't. Now he made some remark about how he'd be glad to get back home.

Leah got up and began to prepare for bed.

The next day they crossed over into Virginia territory.

"Almost home now," Ezra said. "Guess you'll be ready, won't you, Jeff?"

"Sure will." Jeff had insisted on sitting beside Ezra on the wagon seat. He had to hang on, for the road was rutted and he felt lightheaded as well.

Leah was in the back with her father, and Ezra leaned back and said, "In Virginia now, Leah. Mr. Carter, we'll be seeing your uncle pretty soon."

Ten minutes later, they were surprised to see a troop of Confederate infantry marching toward them.

A major on horseback was at the head, and he threw up his hand, stopping the soldiers.

Ezra pulled the horses up short. "Howdy, Major."

The major looked them over carefully and said, "You coming from Sharpsburg?"

Jeff immediately spoke up. "I got sick and couldn't get away with the rest of General Lee's men."

"What's your outfit, boy?"

"Stonewall Brigade. My father is Captain Nelson Majors of Company A."

At once the officer grew more relaxed. "Any more with you, Private?"

"No, sir, just me. These folks are taking me all the way back to Richmond where I hope to find my father. My brother, Tom—he's in the company too."

143

"Well, it was a bad fight. You go on now." He spoke to his men, and they began marching forward.

Ezra slapped the horses with the lines and soon the sound of marching feet faded.

"Well, I guess we're home sure enough if we can see Confederates marching like that," Jeff said.

"Looks pretty good to you, I reckon," Ezra commented.

Jeff hesitated, then said, "Ezra, I have something to tell you."

"Let's have it, Jeff."

Jeff hesitated, then blurted out, "Well, the truth is, I've treated you right bad, Ezra. I was suspicious from the time I saw you there hiding in Silas's barn."

"No reason why you shouldn't be. I was an enemy soldier," Ezra said in a kindly fashion.

"I know, but that wasn't all of it." Jeff bit his lip and let the silence run on for a moment. "Well, hang it all, to tell the truth . . . I guess I've been . . . I hate to say it, Ezra . . ."

"Well, what is it?"

"You see, Leah and me, we've been friends for a long time." Jeff ducked his head, refusing to look at Ezra. "The truth is, it made me a little bit jealous when you and her went hunting birds' eggs. That's always been what me and her have done together."

"Why, you shouldn't feel that way, Jeff," Ezra said. "Leah thinks more of you than she does anybody. She's told me so many times."

"She has?" Jeff brightened and glanced back involuntarily. Some of the tension left his face, and he looked at Ezra. The sun was shining on the boy's curly brown hair. He looked lean and able, his hands big and strong. "Now, that's good of you to say so, Ezra." Awkwardly he stuck his hand over and said, "I'm asking you to forget the way I acted, all right?"

Ezra at once shifted the line to his left hand and shook Jeff's hand cheerfully in a hard grip. "Why, sure. There's no reason me and you can't be friends, is there, Jeff, now that I'm not a Yankee soldier no more?"

"No reason at all."

The wagon trundled down the rutted road, and somehow Jeff felt good—good in the way he'd felt good when he apologized to Lucy. *At least,* he thought finally, *I'm OK with Ezra. Now I've got to tell Leah what a rat I've been—and how much I think of her.*

14

Glad Reunion

The sun was high in the sky when Ezra turned the horses off the main road. They had traveled hard all morning, hoping to reach their destination before noon, and they were only two hours late.

"Wake up, Leah!" Ezra said. "We're here."

Leah, who had been sitting in the wagon seat beside him, came awake with a start. She looked ahead, and her eyes widened with pleasure. She turned and said, "Pa, we're here. Jeff, wake up! We're almost to Uncle Silas's farm."

Ezra directed the team down the dusty road, letting his eyes run over the scene. "Sure never will forget this place, Leah," he said. "My life ain't been the same since I hid out here."

Leah looked fondly at him. "It's funny, isn't it, Ezra? If you'd gone on down the road and hidden in the next barn, we might never have met."

Ezra shook his head. "That would have been bad for me. I'd been caught sooner or later and sent back to Belle Isle Prison."

Leah reached over and patted his wrist. "The Lord always knows what He's doing. That's why He put you at Uncle Silas's house."

Ezra looked down at her hand, which looked very white against his bronzed arm, then glanced away quickly. "Well, I guess we've got a surprise for Mr. Silas, ain't we now?"

After drawing up the team in front of the house, Ezra leaped to the ground, walked around, and put out his hand.

Leah was surprised but took it and stepped lightly to the ground. The two of them went to the back of the wagon then, and Leah stuck her head inside. She saw her father sitting on the cot, smiling.

"We're here, Pa. Come on."

Dan Carter reached over and slapped Jeff on the shoulder. "Come on, boy," he said. "I'm pretty tired of this wagon. It'll be good to have a real bed again and put our feet under a real table."

Ezra and Leah helped the two men down, and Leah said with satisfaction, "You're looking better, Pa."

"I guess a nice travel in a wagon was what I needed. But I give glory to God for His healing." He looked at Jeff and said, "You're looking better too, Jeff. You didn't have much fever last night."

Jeff nodded. With his feet on the ground, he leaned back against the wagon and looked around. "Sure looks good to me. Let's see if your uncle's here."

They went up the steps to the front porch, Jeff hanging onto the pillar as he climbed slowly.

Leah started to take his arm and help but decided not to. Instead she knocked on the door and turned to say, "He's going to be surprised to see you, Pa."

No sooner had she spoken than the door swung open. Silas Carter, wearing a pair of faded overalls, stared at them for one moment in disbelief. Then his face broke into a wide smile. "Well, I swan!" he cried. "Leah, Jeff, and Ezra! What a family reunion! Come in, come in!"

147

"And me too, Uncle Silas." Dan Carter stepped forward and grinned at the surprise and shock that ran across his uncle's face. "Didn't expect to see me, I bet."

Silas Carter appeared to have been struck dumb. He'd not seen this nephew for years. Dan had always been his favorite among his nephews. He'd written him often and had been able to keep up with some of the things Dan had done, especially when Leah and Sarah visited. But now to see him standing on his own front porch—well, evidently he almost couldn't believe it.

"Dan!" Silas cried. He came bursting out the screen door and grabbed his nephew. "Never would've dreamed it!"

The two men hugged, and the three young people grinned at them. Both older men had beards, and it was a little amusing to see them act like schoolboys.

Silas then stepped back and dabbed at his eyes with his shirt sleeve. "You'll have me blubbering like a baby, Dan. Come on in the house and sit."

The five of them were soon seated about the round oak table drinking sassafras tea, and Silas was alternately talking at full speed and demanding answers. As Dan told the story of the battle and how Jeff had been picked up by a Quaker farmer, Silas repeatedly exclaimed, "Well, praise God . . . hallelujah . . . the Lord is good!" He turned around and pounded Jeff's shoulder, saying, "The Lord must favor you, boy." He squeezed his shoulder and said, "You're a little peaked, but some good cooking will take care of that."

"I'll take care of that," Leah said quickly. "I'm tired of cooking over a campfire. Maybe I'll go to

148

town and get a real special treat. You didn't expect a horde of relatives to come barreling in on you, did you?"

"I'm tickled to see you all. But it might be good if you went and picked up a special treat for our celebration," Silas said, stroking his beard thoughtfully. "Let's have a real special supper!"

"I'll go with you," Ezra said. "Help you carry the stuff back."

"No, you'd better not," Leah said. "Somebody might remember you leaving town with me." She didn't mention Lucy's name but saw Jeff give her a quick look.

In the end Leah went by herself to the small store down the road. The shelves were nearly bare, for the South was getting more and more shy of groceries. But there was a luscious dark fruitcake, imported from England.

When Leah paid for the food with a gold coin, the storekeeper's eyes opened wide. "Lawsy, I ain't seen none of these since Hector was a pup! I have to give you your change in Confederate."

"That's all right," Leah said quickly. She took the bundle of Confederate money, knowing it was worth very little, smiled, and went back to Silas's house.

That night they had a fine supper: roast beef, baked potatoes, greens, and cornbread, with two apple pies and slivers of the precious fruitcake for dessert.

Afterward, both Dan and Jeff were tired, and Silas had Ezra set up cots and make pallets here and there.

Dan Carter and Uncle Silas looked at each other before Dan went to bed, and Dan said, "I've never forgotten how you took care of me and my family when we needed it, Silas."

"Well, now I can do something for you again," Silas said fondly. "You go to bed now. We've got a lot of talking to do tomorrow."

And soon the house grew quiet.

When Ezra had gone up to bed in the loft, Jeff lay down wearily on the cot set up for him in the living room.

Suddenly Leah came in. She brought a thin quilt with her and said, "It's pretty warm now, but sometimes it gets cool before morning, Jeff."

Jeff stood up and took the quilt. He knew the time had come.

"Leah," he said, "I'm sure sorry about the way I treated you in Kentucky."

Leah looked at him. "We were both wrong, Jeff. I don't know why we have to fuss. It's no fun, is it?"

"No, it's not." He managed a shy grin. "Best of friends, aren't we?"

Leah put out her hand. "Always the best of friends, Jeff. That's what we always say, isn't it? I couldn't have borne it if I hadn't found you and been able to make things right between us."

Jeff wanted to say more, but she turned and left the room. He sat down on the cot and looked out the window. The partially visible moon was sailing by, dragging filmy clouds after it. He watched for a while and then drew in a satisfied breath, lay back, and went into the first good night's rest he'd had since he'd gotten sick.

The next day after breakfast Leah said, "Come

on, Jeff. You need to get some sunshine. You look like the underside of a catfish."

He laughed and got up from the table. "You sure know how to make a fellow feel good, Leah."

However, he was glad to get outside. The sun shone brightly, and there was a slight breeze that cooled his face. "Sure is good to be out of that wagon," he said. "And to get over being sick." He kicked a stone and watched as it skittered across the road. Then he walked over to the rail fence where clematis was still blooming, picked one of the blossoms, and said, "Always was partial to clematis. Real delicate like."

"I like it too," Leah said. "But I like the little violets down by the creek in the spring the best. The wild kind that grow with the moss out in the deep woods. Wish we could find enough today to make a little bouquet."

They did not find violets, but they had a fine walk. When they headed back and came in sight of the house, Leah said, "Look, there's a buggy!"

Jeff at once recognized it. "That's the Driscolls' buggy, I think."

"The Driscolls'?" Leah sounded shocked. "What is Mr. Driscoll coming for? To see Uncle Silas, I guess."

Jeff did not answer. He had not told Leah about Lucy. There had not been time for that, but he decided to make up for it now, as well as he could, in case Lucy had come along—though he couldn't imagine how she could know he had returned. "Leah, I have to tell you—before I left here, I got to be kind of friends with Lucy."

Leah stopped dead still. *"Friends?* With *that* girl? After what she did? How could you?"

151

Jeff said hastily, "I know. I was about as mad as you. She was wrong to tell that captain about Ezra. But she told me she was sorry."

Leah's face was stiff with anger. "Sorry? A lot of good that would have done if Ezra had been caught. And we might've been hanged as spies!"

Jeff kicked at the dust, not knowing what to say. "Well," he said slowly, "she did say she was sorry. I went to church with Uncle Silas, and her folks invited us home. After that Lucy and I had a little talk." He turned to look at her. "You know, I think I discovered something from having that fight with you, Leah. It taught me it doesn't do any good staying mad at people."

But his words seemed to flow over Leah's head. He knew she had been furious with Lucy. She had never liked the girl, and her dislike came perhaps from personal reasons. She had never forgotten how Lucy had made fun of her at the birthday party.

Now she said, "She's spoiled. She always has to have her own way."

"I expect some of that's so," Jeff agreed. "But anyway, she said she was wrong to do what she did. What could I do? I had to say it was all right—that I forgave her. Isn't that what your father would have done?"

By this time they had reached the porch, and as they entered the house, Lucy jumped up, saying, "Jeff!" Her eyes were bright. She was wearing an attractive white dress trimmed in green lace. She looked very pretty coming up to him.

"I've been stopping by Uncle Silas's house almost every day, hoping he'd heard from you. Imagine my delight when he told me you were actually

152

here! I'm so glad you're back. I was so afraid that you'd been shot or something awful."

"Nope, just got sick." Jeff grinned shyly. Then he turned and said, "If it hadn't been for Leah here and . . . another friend . . . I guess I never would've made it. They took care of me and Mr. Carter all the way back from the battle."

Lucy turned with a smile to Leah, but when she saw the stony expression on the girl's face she halted abruptly. "Well," she said slowly. "That was very nice of you and Ezra, Leah." She bit her lip, then said, "I want to tell you how sorry I am for what I did. It was awful!" Then she tried to smile. "I hope we can see more of each other. At least we have Jeff in common!"

"I doubt that." Leah shrugged, leaving unclear whether she doubted their future social engagements or that she was willing to share Jeff. "I'll be pretty busy taking care of things around here." She moved closer to Jeff, touching his sleeve possessively.

Lucy turned pale, and her eyes went to Jeff's face.

Jeff dropped his head and shrugged his shoulders. He whispered to Lucy, "Leave her alone. She'll have to discover what's the right thing to do just like I did, Lucy."

Lucy gave no hint that she had heard Jeff but turned to the assembled group and said quietly, "I'll have to be going. Good-bye, Mr. Carter—nice to have met you. Uncle Silas, good to see you." She went out the door, and there was an uncomfortable silence.

Everyone looked at Leah, and she flushed. "Well," she said stubbornly, "I know I wasn't very

153

nice. But how do we know that she won't run right to that Wesley Lyons and tell him that Ezra's here? She did it before."

Jeff said, "She already told me she was sorry about that, Leah. And nobody's told her Ezra is here. I don't think she'll do anything. She's a pretty nice young lady."

But Leah said, "I don't trust her."

She flounced off to the kitchen, and Ezra came in and looked at Jeff. He'd stayed out of the living room, and his presence hadn't been mentioned by the Carters the whole time Lucy had visited. Ezra was still cautious.

Nodding in the direction Leah had stomped, Ezra remarked, "I guess she's pretty mad. I wish she wasn't, though. It's not good for her, even if Lucy isn't very predictable."

Dan Carter looked toward the kitchen where his daughter had disappeared. "Yep, she's wrong this time. But nobody can talk to Leah. She's as stubborn as a blue-nosed mule when she gets her back up. We'll all just have to pray for her." He sighed heavily. "It sure is hard to raise a daughter."

15
Lucy Saves the Day

Everything went well at the home of Silas Carter for the next two days—except that Leah was impossible. Jeff tried more than once to get close to her, but it never worked.

"She's not mad at me anymore," he said to her father. "But she just can't get over the way she feels about Lucy Driscoll."

"I know," Mr. Carter said regretfully. "I've tried to talk to her about it. All she'll do is squint her eyes and shake her head and say that Lucy's not to be trusted."

"Looks like she'd realize that if Lucy did know Ezra's here and was going to turn him in, she would've done it already."

"Well, when people let anger and bitterness get in them, they do foolish things." Dan shifted in his rocking chair and looked down at the piece of cedar he'd been whittling. The shavings made a sweet-smelling pile at his feet. "Always did like the smell of fresh-cut cedar," he murmured. He sent another curled shaving to the floor. "We've got to do something about her, boy. She's just dead wrong."

Later in the day Ezra made another appeal to Leah. The two of them were out looking for guinea hen eggs in the sprawling hen yard. Leah seemed to be enjoying the sunshine and being outside. "These

155

guineas think every day's Easter, hiding their eggs like they do." She laughed. "I don't see how they remember where they are themselves."

"Here's one." Ezra reached into a pocket of dried grass and drew forth a small egg. He stared at it, holding it between his thumb and forefinger. Then he grinned. "Take a lot of these to make a dozen, wouldn't it?"

Leah laughed. "You're crazy, Ezra. But it would take a lot to feed an appetite like yours."

They continued to search for eggs until finally Leah said, "I guess this is all we're going to find. Maybe there'll be enough for an omelet for Pa and Uncle Silas."

Ezra stood loosely in the sunlight, his face re-laxed. His eyes were reflective, and he said, "You know, I remember what I was like when you found me the first time. Skinny as a rail, sick and hardly able to hold my head up. I think about that a lot, Leah."

Leah turned to face him. "I'm glad I did find you, Ezra," she said softly.

"You're the kindest girl I ever saw."

"Oh, I am not."

"Sure you are." Ezra hesitated, then said, "I guess it's not my place to say so, but I hate to see you feeling like you do about Lucy."

At once Leah's face grew tense. "You don't know her, Ezra," she said. "She's spoiled. She learned how to fool her parents probably when she was a year old. She's been doing what she pleased ever since. She knows how to fool other people too. I've seen her. The boys fall all over themselves to make her happy—and that's what she's doing to you and Jeff. You're just too blind to see it!"

Ezra shoved his straw hat back, and his curly hair fell over his forehead. He fingered the brass buckle at his waist for a moment uncertainly, then shook his head. "I don't doubt she's spoiled. She's the only child of rich parents—and a pretty girl. It'd be a wonder if she wasn't." He suddenly dropped his hand and looked directly at Leah. "But that's no reason she can't be sorry for a mistake, just like us poor ugly folks."

He tried to grin to make his words softer but saw the stubbornness on Leah's face. "Well," he said, "I'm not going to say anything else about it. I know you'll think better of the way you've been acting."

"I've been acting just right!" Leah said sharply. Then she forced herself to smile. "Come on, let's go down the road. I want to show you where the big woodpecker lives. He's three times as big as a red-headed woodpecker and has a striped back and has a tuft of a feather on his head. I don't know how to tell you. Come on."

Ezra and Leah walked down the road. They passed several wagons, but were so engrossed in their conversation that they did not notice that one wagon was driven by Rufus Prather, the overgrown boy hired by the Driscolls.

Rufus Prather was fat and lazy and totally untrustworthy. He'd been the instrument of almost getting Ezra captured. He had been soundly reprimanded by his employer for that. And when he saw Ezra he recognized him instantly.

"It's that escaped Yankee prisoner!" he whispered to himself. His little eyes glinted, and he said angrily, "This time we'll get him for sure!"

He whipped up the horses and made his way into Richmond, where he found Captain Wesley Lyons in his office.

"Captain Lyons, you know that Yankee soldier that escaped? The one that got away with Leah Carter?"

Lyons was a tall man with brown hair and a rather childish face. He'd had bad experiences with both Sarah Carter and Leah. Now he turned and said abruptly, "There wasn't anyone with her except Jeff Majors. You made a mess out of it and got me in trouble with the colonel."

"But," Prather said, "you can get him this time. I seen him plain as day, and he didn't see me."

"All right, where is he?" Captain Lyons demanded.

"He's at Silas Carter's place. I seen him walking along the road with Leah Carter. You can get them this time, Captain. I'll bet you can."

Captain Lyons rubbed his chin thoughtfully, and a smile turned up the corners of his thin lips. "All right, I'll see to it. Now get out of here."

Rufus left at once, and all the way home he enjoyed thinking about his revenge when he would see the Yankee soldier caught and Leah humiliated, even arrested as a spy.

"That'll show her she ain't too good for me," he chortled. Then he said, "Git up, horse."

He arrived at the Driscoll house and was unhitching the horse when Lucy came in from her afternoon ride on her small gray mare.

"Miss Lucy," he said excitedly. "Guess what? We're going to get them this time."

Lucy had not yet dismounted. She said, "Get who?"

"That Yankee prisoner. I seen him and Leah Carter walking down the road."

"You must've made a mistake, Rufus."

"No," Rufus insisted. "I seen them—it was them, and I done told Captain Lyons. We'll get them this time. That'll be something, won't it? Last time they got away from us, but we'll get them this time!"

Lucy smiled and said, "I expect so. Captain Lyons will take care of it." She did not dismount but said, "I think I'll ride a bit more. My mare's not tired yet." She turned her horse and rode out of the yard at a fast walk.

As soon as Lucy was out of sight of the house, she said, "Come on, girl! Let's see how fast you can go now." She rode at a gallop to the house down the road. It was a tall, two-story home belonging to the Taylors. She drew up, and when a maid came out to inquire, she called, "Is Cecil here?"

"Yes, ma'am, he here. I'll send him right out." The maid turned and walked back inside.

Soon Cecil Taylor came out the door. "What is it, Lucy?"

Lucy said, "Come on, Cecil, get your horse! Hurry!"

"What for? Where we going?"

"I'll explain to you on the way. Hurry up! We've got to go as fast as we can."

Leah was setting the table for supper when she looked out the window and was startled. "Well, what does she want?" she muttered under her breath.

159

Jeff, who had been sitting at the table, got up and walked to the window. "I know him. That's Cecil Taylor. And Lucy . . ." He watched the pair approach and said, "They're riding like Old Scratch is after them. What's their hurry, I wonder?"

Now Ezra came to peer over Leah's shoulder as the horses thundered into the yard. "Well, they're coming here—and look how them horses are lathered! There must be something wrong."

The three of them were turning to go to the door when it burst open, and Lucy and Cecil ran in.

"Ezra, you've got to get away!" Lucy cried. "Captain Lyons knows you're here. He's coming after you!"

Leah stared at the girl. "I *knew* she would tell them! I just knew she would!"

But Cecil Taylor turned his bright blue eyes on her. "You're wrong about that. It was Rufus. Rufus told the captain, and then Rufus told Lucy." His voice was accusing, and he said, "I'm surprised you'd think such a thing, Leah."

Leah was stopped dead in her tracks, but she had no time to say more.

Lucy said, "They're expecting to see a stranger here. Get away as quick as you can, Ezra. That's what I brought Cecil for. When Captain Lyons comes, he'll find him here and not you."

Dan Carter, who'd said nothing so far, now spoke up. "Lucy's right. You've got to get out of here, Ezra. Take one of the horses and head on out. Hide out until dark. This ain't safe territory for you."

Ezra obviously did not want to go, but when Silas said, "You've got to do it, boy. You can come

160

back later when things have cooled down," he finally gave in.

"All right." Ezra ran out the door and was saddling a horse when Leah came into the barn. "Don't get caught, Ezra. I couldn't stand it if something happened to you after all of this."

"I'll be all right," Ezra said. He took the reins and threw them over the horse's neck. Before he swung into the saddle, he said, "You'll be all right, won't you?"

"Yes, I will, but you be careful."

Ezra said, "You feel any different about Lucy?"

Leah's face was pale, and she nodded. "I was wrong about her." Tears came to her eyes. "I guess I've been wrong about everybody."

Ezra gave her a quick hug, the first time he'd ever done so. He smiled down at her, saying, "You're the kindest girl I ever met, Leah Carter. Don't you ever forget it." He swung into the saddle, then rode out of the barn as Leah stood watching.

She saw him go into the woods, and no sooner had he disappeared than six mounted men came from the other direction. Leah went into the house, saying, "They're coming!"

"Here—sit down, everybody. We're eating supper just like nothing's happened," Uncle Silas said.

They all took their places, and soon a knock came at the door. When Leah opened it, she said, "Well, Captain Lyons, how nice to see you again."

Captain Lyons glared at her. "I'm not here on a social visit. Is your uncle here?"

"Why, yes, right over here. Come in."

Lyons stepped inside and looked around the room. "We've had reports that there's an escaped prisoner here. I'll have to search the place."

"Why, of course, Captain. You go right ahead and search," Uncle Silas said. "I don't believe you've met my nephew, Dan Carter. He's Leah's pa."

"Glad to know you."

Dan Carter smiled and said, "I believe you met my older daughter, Sarah, on her last visit. And of course you know Cecil here."

Anger ran across the officer's face, and he did not answer. He turned and said, "Sergeant, search the barn and all the outbuildings. I'll search the house."

For the next thirty minutes, the patrol searched every inch of the farm, while Captain Wesley Lyons did everything but look under the mattresses. Finally he came with a red face to say, "If you see any strangers, I want to be informed. You understand me?"

"Oh, yes, I've always understood you," Uncle Silas said cheerfully. He winked at Leah. "If we see any escaped prisoners, we'll sure report them. Won't we, Leah?"

"Yes, we will, Uncle Silas."

Lyons glared at them and went outside, slamming the door.

The sergeant was waiting for him on the porch and said, "We didn't find nothing, sir. How about you?"

"No, it was that fool Rufus again. Nobody there but Cecil Taylor. I think I'll take a strap to that Rufus Prather. Anybody that can't tell an escaped Yankee prisoner from Cecil Taylor deserves a strapping. Let's go."

Inside, Jeff stood at the window until they were gone. Then he turned. "We're all right. They're gone." He smiled warmly at Cecil, saying, "Thanks for coming, Cecil. You saved our bacon this time."

"Naw," Cecil drawled, "I reckon not. It was Lucy here. I wouldn't have known a thing if she hadn't come for me."

Lucy said, "Well, I'm glad Ezra got away. I'd hate to see him in a prison camp again."

Leah sat there, her face pale, looking down at the table and saying not a word.

16

Parting Is
Such Sweet Sorrow

Never had Leah felt so miserable. Two days had passed since Lucy Driscoll and Cecil Taylor saved Ezra from being captured. Now it was time to think about going back to Kentucky.

Her father had said, "Your ma needs us there, and we've got to get back. We'll leave in two days, maybe."

Leah had agreed but was unhappy. For some reason she had been unable to apologize to Lucy. No one had talked to her about it, but she sensed that everyone was disappointed in her.

When Lucy was around, Leah had been polite but had hardly spoken to her. Perhaps this had something to do with the fact that Jeff apparently found Lucy an attractive young lady. The two of them laughed a lot; and the more they laughed, the more Leah seemed to freeze up.

On the day before their departure, Leah went for a long walk in the woods. She filled a basket with wild flowers, and ordinarily this would have pleased her, but she was unhappy. Finally she started home.

Suddenly, from behind a large elm, Ezra stepped out in front of Leah. "Good thing I wasn't a wild Indian," he said, his white teeth showing. "I could've scalped you."

"There haven't been any Indians around here for a long time," Leah muttered.

Ezra walked along with her, speaking of unimportant things, but finally he reached out and took her arm. "Leah," he said, "I've got to talk to you."

"You don't have to hold onto me. I'm not going to run away."

Ezra dropped her arm but shook his head. "Everybody is worried about you," he said simply. "Your pa's worried sick. He says he's never seen you act this way before."

"There's nothing wrong with me."

"Yes, there is," Ezra said almost harshly. "You're just not yourself—and everybody knows what the trouble is too."

"I don't have any trouble. You're all imagining things."

"That's not so." Ezra took a deep breath. "You're all sullened up like a 'possum, and you're jealous of Lucy Driscoll."

"Jealous?" Leah's green eyes flashed. "You're crazy, Ezra. I'm not jealous of anybody."

"You're giving a good imitation of it then. You ought to see yourself when Jeff's talking to her."

"I don't want to listen to any more of this." Leah turned to walk off, but he grasped her arm again. "Let me go!"

"No, I won't. You helped me when nobody else would. Now I don't care how bad it hurts you—I'm going to tell you about yourself."

Ordinarily there was no milder-mannered young man than Ezra Payne, but for the next five minutes he stood there holding onto Leah's arm, telling her exactly how she was behaving.

Finally he said, "I hate to talk to you like this, Leah. You're my friend, but being a friend with somebody means you sometimes have to tell them the truth even if it hurts. And the truth is that it's not Lucy acting like a spoiled brat—it's you."

Leah had kept her head down for some time, enduring Ezra's words. Suddenly her shoulders began to shake, and Ezra bent over to see tears running down her cheeks.

"Oh, yikes—don't cry, Leah! Please don't cry!"

Leah fell against Ezra and clung to him and began sobbing like a baby.

Not knowing what else to do, Ezra held her and patted her shoulder awkwardly.

Finally the spasm ceased, and she stepped back. She took a handkerchief from her pocket and wiped her face. "You're right, Ezra," she said simply. "Pa's right, and Jeff's right, and so is Uncle Silas. I've acted like a spoiled brat, and I need a whipping!" Her lips were drawn tight, and there was determination in her face. "But it's all over. I'm going to tell Lucy I'm sorry."

"Well . . . er . . . well, I think that'll be great. You want me to go with you?"

"No, this is between me and her." She then tried to smile and said, "Thank you, Ezra. I know it took a lot of courage to tell me off like that. You just don't like to fuss at anybody, do you?"

"I really don't," he admitted. "But I'm glad you're going to make it right with Lucy. I'll wait here in the woods. Jeff said he's going to come out. Maybe we'll go fishing in the pond."

Ezra never learned what happened between Lucy and Leah—nor did anyone else.

All afternoon he stayed in the shadow of the big trees, and finally, a little after three, he heard voices. Slipping through the trees, he glanced down the path, and his heart leaped when he saw Leah and Lucy. Jeff was with them too.

"Must have made it all right," he said with a sigh of relief. Coming out of the trees, he said, "Hey, where are you three headed?"

Jeff held up several poles made out of saplings. "Going to catch the biggest fish in the creek. I can outfish anyone here."

Leah said at once, "You never could beat me fishing, Jeff Majors!"

Jeff grinned at her. "Our usual bet then. The one that catches the least fish cleans them all."

"That's a bet," Leah said. "Not a bet really, because I never lose. It's a sure thing."

Lucy was, for once, wearing a pair of overalls. They were not made for a man, however, but cut to fit her. She had a straw hat on and looked a little out of place not wearing a fancy dress. "You two fish a lot?" she asked.

"Oh, sure, Lucy, but I always beat him. You'll beat him too."

Lucy said, "I don't know how to fish. I've never tried it."

Ezra said, "*I* have. I'm the fishingest man you ever saw. I'll even put the worms on your hook."

Lucy came over to stand beside Ezra. "That's good," she said with a slight shiver. "I think they're nasty."

The boys laughed, but Leah said, "Don't let them make fun of you." She smiled at Lucy, and

Lucy smiled back. "Come on. You and I will catch more fish than these two overgrown babies."

"Hey, that'll be the bet then. If you two catch more fish than we do," Jeff said, "Ezra and I will clean all the fish. Otherwise you two'll do it."

Leah took up the challenge at once. "Yes, we'll show you a thing or two. Come on, Lucy."

It was a fine afternoon. The girls stayed together laughing, and Lucy finally learned to thread a worm on a hook.

When the two boys went farther up the creek, looking for bigger fish, Ezra said, "I guess Leah's OK."

"Yes, it's good to have her back again," Jeff said warmly. "She wasn't herself, but she's fine now. I guess it just took her longer than me to discover what I did—forgiveness makes you feel a whole lot better than holding a grudge!"

It was late when they got back to the house. Uncle Silas and Dan Carter were on the porch. "Who caught the most fish?" Silas demanded.

"We did—Lucy and me," Leah said at once.

Jeff said indignantly, "It wasn't fair. They kept every little old fish they got. Ezra and I only kept those big enough to eat."

Lucy said, "Nothing was said about size. We caught forty-two fish, and you only caught twelve."

"Some of those little old fish you could put in your eye and not even blink!" Ezra complained. "But a bet's a bet. Come on, Jeff, let's clean fish."

They had a fine supper of fried fish, hush puppies, fried potatoes, and fresh baked pie. Later in the evening, Jeff and Leah slipped out to watch the moon rise over the haystacks.

"It was a good day, wasn't it, Jeff?" she whispered.

"Sure was." He wanted to say something about Lucy but didn't want to offend her. Instead he said, "I guess you and Ezra and Mr. Carter will be heading back. I hate to see you go."

"Seems like we're always saying good-bye, doesn't it?"

He reached over and took her hand. Her eyes were luminous in the moonlight. She said nothing, but he felt the warmth of her hand as he held it.

Jeff looked at her fondly. "My pa said something once. He said Christians never really say good-bye."

Leah smiled warmly, her full lips curving upwards. "I like that."

"I don't know what it means exactly." He gave her hand a final squeeze, then released it. "But don't be surprised if I show up on your doorstep in Kentucky pretty soon." He cleared his throat. "I've got to see my baby sister, don't I?"

Leah reached out and pushed his hair back where it had fallen over his forehead. She asked softly, "Is it just Esther you're coming to see, Jeff?"

He looked down at his feet, then looked up at her and grinned. "No, there's somebody else in Kentucky that I'll be coming to see too."

The moon rose high, a silver disk shedding its beams down on the field. A raccoon, masked like a burglar, came out of the woods, headed for the cornfield for his nightly raid. He stopped and peered in alarm at the two young people, but they stood very still. Then he moved into the darkness and was gone.

169